Copyright © 2023 John H Mallett

All rights reserved

The characters and events portrayed in this book are fictitious. Any similarity to real persons, living or dead, is coincidental and not intended by the author.

No part of this book may be reproduced, or stored in a retrieval system, or transmitted in any form or by any means, electronic, mechanical, photocopying, recording, or otherwise, without express written permission of the publisher.

Cover design by: J Mallett

Pre edit author copy!
John.

HARRISON FILES

INTO A CONSPIRACY WITHOUT KNOWING.

CHAPTER 1

A NORMAL DAY AT THE OFFICE?

It was a warm August day. At least, it was warm for Tulsa. It would have been steaming hot for anyone not used to 98 degrees. It had taken me three years before I had got out of the habit of going from one air-conditioned building to the next and running the car air-conditioning at maximum during the summer.

The tarmac of the airport roads and taxi-ways were shimmering, so that it was difficult to see the plane on the runway taking off until it got quite a long way into the air. I parked the Chevy van and strolled across the road towards the flying club building. It was a low temporary looking building, like many on the smaller airfields in the USA.

Another tradition seems to be the three or four plastic chairs next to the entrance, on the sandy excuse for grass, which is also unique to this latitude. In the chair closest to the door was a well built man, with sandy hair and slightly dusty jeans, in his late thirties. He sat, or should I say, lay with his feet in one chair and his neck resting on the back of the other. A can of diet Coke in one hand and a straw hat in the other used as a fan.

'Hi Jon, another hot one,' was his greeting as he allowed the condensation on the Coke can to drip onto his forehead.

'Yes, it is Chuck, nobody flying today?' I replied.

As I walked towards the door, he got up and followed me into the entrance. Inside it was cool, but there was the added distraction of the noise from several air-conditioning units, that were clearly struggling to maintain a comfortable temperature. Chuck walked around a small counter area and peered into a large well-used book.

'Well, where you off to today?' he said running his finger down the page.

'You didn't book!' he exclaimed, staring at me with a puzzled expression.

'No, I just took a chance as it was early in the afternoon and quite hot, I thought you might have a spare one-seventy-two,' I explained with an enquiring expression. I was trying to read the page upside down.

There were times in one hour slots down one side of the page with lines and names written in the next column. The next few columns were headed with the letter N and a number that was the aircraft registration number. It was also of significant interest to a pilot that the further Chucks eyes went across the page the more expensive the aircraft was per hour.

After some seconds of turning his head sideways to read the untidy and badly placed lines, he exclaimed, 'OK, ther y' go.'

He spun the book around with his finger on the intersection of a time and an aircraft column.

'It's six seven echo, over by the pumps.'

I drew a line below his finger and wrote my name in the space. He spun the book round again and looked seriously at me, as if a world secret was going to be imparted.

'Ya know where the keys go, when you get back now,' he said quietly pointing at the top shelf of a book case, that was well above eye height.

'Sure, I've got back late at night quite a few times,' I replied.

Nowhere was very safe in the airport buildings, despite the security patrol. It was Chuck's habit to regularly change the location of aircraft keys that were returned after he had gone home. Chuck went to a small cash box on the counter and took out some keys. He read the tags' one by one and eventually found the one he was looking for and threw it to me in a slow over arm. I only just caught it and in the process nearly knocked over his Coke.

'Well, have a good flight,' he said smiling.

I waved and thanked him as I walked out into the heat.

As I stopped at the van to pick up my flight bag, Jim was just pulling up in his car. We had known each other for some years and worked in the same small electronics company. He had managed to stay the same wiry fit looking man as he was when

I first met him in England. I had always wondered how someone who enjoyed his steak, cigarettes and beer had managed this, while I just seemed to put on weight without drinking that much beer and eating at the health food store.

'Are you ready then?' he said giving me a very solid hand shake. He was always very excited about flying and took every opportunity to take a trip with me to pick up some parts or deliver some urgent drawings for the company. On this occasion we were going to McAlester to pick up some drawings that had been produced by a subcontractor. It would be a flight of about an hour and I had phoned for the weather and filed a flight plan from home. The weather indicated some scattered cloud at 6000 feet but no indication of anything more serious. However, cautious pilots spend some time looking out for small but violent storms and even tornado's that are common in the Tulsa area during summer. It was only a couple of years ago that a whole town had been destroyed in such a tornado.

Jim and I walked to the plane that was parked on a small tarmac area next to two small fuel pumps. Next to the Cessna 172 aeroplane was a small set of metal steps. On the steps was balanced a boy who did not look old enough to know where to put the fuel. In fact, he had been around aeroplanes all of his life. He wore a blue boiler suit and a baseball cap. He had just finished refuelling the plane and ensuring that the tank caps were correctly fitted.

'OK Sir, twenty-one in each tank, oil OK, no reported problems,' he stated with a professional manner as he slid down the ladder. He folded the ladder and walked over to put the lock back on the pumps and stow the ladder between the two pumps.

'Have a good flight,' he said as he walked towards the building.

Despite the assurance and professionalism of the boy, I always made a point of checking the plane myself. Not that I would not wish to take a calculated risk, but I always felt that it was only a few minutes and you cannot get out and check anything once you get off the ground. Anyway, I had always liked aeroplanes and took any legitimate opportunity to fix a potential problem before it became serious.

We opened both the doors to let the heat out

of the cockpit. I turned on the master switch and lowered the flaps. After my pre-flight walk around the plane checking nuts, pins, control surfaces, oil and fuel, I took one last look around under the plane and climbed in the left door. Jim was already reading the chart and folding it to a manageable size. I organised the cockpit and filled in the information from air traffic on my flight plan before I shouted, 'Clear of the prop,' and started the engine.

Once our headsets were on we could talk in a normal voice and the engine was a low whine in the background. We got clearance to taxi and fastened our lap belts. Jim fanned himself with the chart. It was hot on the ground with the doors shut and even with the vents open only the occasional small puff of air would cool the sweat on your brow. Taxiing brought a little more air and checking the engine and magnetos seemed to bring an air of anticipation that stopped the concern about the heat. We would soon be climbing into the cooler air.

'Six seven echo, clear for take-off,' the controller said in a monotone voice.

I replied 'six seven echo clear for take-off,'

and after peering out of the side window for any possible traffic, pulled onto the runway and eased the throttle to full power. We got into the air and climbed away from the ground.

The early part of the flight was under the control of the radar and I was quite busy selecting frequencies and radar transponder codes that allow the radar to identify the aircraft and its altitude. We flew south on our course, climbing to 5500 ft. It was now cool and the scene all around was without feature. Jim liked to know the flight plan and the check points and would point to them as we progressed. The landscape was without many reference points as the roads divided the green or should I say grey areas up into squares all the same size. The green of the fields became greyer as we climbed up to altitude. Jim had done this route a number of times and filled in the time on the flight plan as we passed the ground reference town or lake. Navigation on this trip was not very difficult in good weather because the highway was visible out of Jim's window for the entire flight.

We were soon approaching McAlester and

calling our approach on the radio. However, there was no other traffic and we made a normal pass over the airfield above the pattern height to check the wind sock. We were now down to 1800ft and the runway was out of the window to our left. The plane began to hit some turbulence as I turned onto final approach. With the runway ahead I lowered more flap, corrected for the small crosswind and removed some power. Jim began putting the charts and calculator in the flight bag in an air of confidence and I think to distract him from the pitching horizon.

The Cessna bumped around in the turbulent air near the ground and Jim looked a little tense but looked at me and smiled. We had been in much rougher conditions and he could see that I was not concerned. Once I was within a few feet of the ground the plane stopped bucking and smoothed as if we had entered a vacuum. Finally, shuffling onto the runway I braked and turned onto the first taxi way on the right, heading to the buildings. Once again the heat was building and by the time we parked I was glad to get the doors open.

The airport was significantly smaller than

Riverside, our starting point. It had good facilities including taxis and even rental cars if requested. Jim had booked a taxi and it was planned that he would be back at about 21:00. That gave me a couple of hours to relax before I filed a flight plan back. I found the drinks machine and got a couple of cans of Coke. I had the plane topped up with fuel and found a chair and some local papers, then proceeded to look for a cool place to relax. The sun was not so hot now and a light breeze was blowing from the South-West. I decided to sit outside and watch the sun go down. It felt good to drink the cold Coke and I could not stop until it had all gone.

The local paper was full of news about the local events, like how well the baseball team were doing and charity fund raising. On the second page was a couple of inches of text that caught my interest. It was headed, 'Pollution, is it changing our weather'. It reported that town records had seen a marked increase in the number of sudden storms and tornados, over the past few years. I remember thinking to myself that this was more likely the sunspot cycle. This has a cyclic effect on our weather of about 21 years that is just long enough for people to forget the last time they had weather like this. However, there were some peculiarities that stuck in my mind. One of these was that the same house had been struck by lightning three times. The last strike had burnt it to the ground.

'Hello,' said a soft voice. I jumped! That strange feeling you get when woken from a deep sleep, as if you have just stepped back into your body. It was a woman of about thirty with long dark hair and brown eyes. She was dressed in a thin short sleeved shirt and jeans. In my suddenly awakened state it was an instant impression that she was very attractive with a lovely figure.

'Sorry, I didn't mean to startle you,' she said in a voice like warm chocolate over ice cream. Pulling myself together and back into reality, while trying not to make it obvious that I was smoothing down my hair I said,

'Hello, where did you come from?'

Which I realised was a stupid thing to say, almost as the words came out, but I had just woken up. She looked at me more intently.

'Where are you from? With that accent you're not from Oklahoma.'

'No,' I said. 'I'm from England.'

'Oh,' she said with a slightly distant tone.

'Are you a visiting student pilot?'

I was now more awake and aware that this was more than a passing interest.

'No, I live in Tulsa and I fly down here quite often.'

She sat down in front of me on the grass with her arms behind her and her legs crossed.

'Do you work on the airport,' I asked.

'No, I live over there and I usually go for a walk in the evenings,' she pointed to an area behind the airport buildings. I could not help looking at her large brown eyes and her smile that seemed to radiate from her whole face.

'My name is Jon Harrison,' I said leaning forward and holding out my hand.

'OK, mine is Lorna,' she said as she grabbed my hand with a strong grip.

We talked about the area of McAlester and my home in England. She had lived here since she left University in Oklahoma. She worked in the oil industry studying the geology of the area, all over Texas and Oklahoma. She had a detailed knowledge of the terrain and sub terrain of a very wide area. I told her about my jobs in Canada,

New York and England. I explained why I had come to Tulsa to grow a small Company into a high technology electronics design business, the challenge and satisfaction, when it comes together.

It was getting colder now, which is quite common in locations that have a very clear sky. The haze that existed during the heat of the day had now gone and the only remaining evidence of the heat was the twinkling stars. Lorna was now lying on the grass staring at the stars. Because there were no street lights it seemed that the whole sky was a mass of twinkling lights, some seemed close and some in the distance. It was only just possible to see the area of sky where the sun had gone down. The new moon was now below the horizon and this made the landscape seem very dark.

We spent some time comparing knowledge about the constellations and individual stars. On this occasion I had met my match. Suddenly she jumped to her feet and brushed the grass from her jeans.

'I must get on my way home,' she said with a smile.

'It is getting late!' she exclaimed using a lighter to look at her watch.

'Shall I walk with you down to the road?' I said as I got up from my chair.

'You don't have to, I know this airfield very well.'

I explained that I would feel happier knowing that she was in sight of her house. We set off at a brisk pace, heading round some buildings and down the airport access road.

Some headlights soon came down the road and went past us slowly, then stopped. A voice called out from the dark.

'Jon! Come on, jump in.'

Lorna said, 'You go, it's been nice talking to you.'

I was very firm and said 'We will run you home in the taxi.'

I shouted to Jim to hold on and as I turned she was already following me. I opened the door next to Jim and we all climbed in the back.

'You give the driver directions,' I whispered to Lorna.

The car reversed into a small gateway and Lorna leaned forward and was pointing and giving directions to the driver. Jim smiled at me, with one of those, I know what you've been up to, smiles. We soon reached her house, or at least I think we did, because it was hidden by trees. I opened the door and held it for her to get out.

I instantly said,

'I really enjoyed your company, I hope we meet again. Oh! Jim have you got a pen?' I exclaimed turning back to the car. He pulled one out of my top pocket and threw me another smile. He dug his hand into his jacket and handed me one of his business cards. I wrote my phone number on the back with 'Jon from Tulsa.' Handing it to her, I said. 'Call me if you come up to Tulsa.'

She waved as she walked away and said 'You never know I might just do that! Byeee,'

Jim and I climbed back into the cab and Jim leaned over to the driver and said, 'airport main entrance please.'

It was only a minute or two before we arrived at the front of the airport building. Jim thrust some notes into the drivers hand and he said, 'Thank you and you have a good flight now!'

I explained to Jim that I had been a bit busy and had not completed my flight plan or called for the weather yet.

'Well you go and do the paper work while I find a coffee machine,' he said in a slightly sarcastic tone and a grin on his face as he walked into the building.

I found the phone for the weather report. I had to listen to the forecast twice due to not paying enough attention the first time. I said to myself 'wake up now!'

Having completed the planning I went out to the plane and performed a more than detailed pre-flight check.

We completed the checks and were soon at full power, lifting off the ground and in a very smooth climb to altitude. The visibility was very good and even though the moon was not lighting the land, it was easy to see the streets and the highway. We were just past McAlester lake when I first saw a flash of lightning off to our left by about 10 degrees.

'That looks like quite a storm,' Jim said pointing over the instrument panel.

'Well, I had better take a little deviation.'

I banked the plane to the right until the activity was out to the left. We continued to watch the storm as it got bigger and more active.

There were strange violet flashes and then,

'Jon look at that!' Jim said as he leaned over my chest and stared out of my window.

'I see it!' I shouted.

It was like a fireball travelling towards us but lower. It seemed to be travelling in a straight line. Then it hit something, showering flames and fire in all directions. 'Wow!' said Jim, looking at me in the light of the instrument panel. All we could see of the explosion now was a very small fire and what seemed to be a violet glow, the trail of the fireball. The trail was very faint and it vanished as fast as it had appeared.

I had heard of ball lightning, but never seen it. For some reason I thought it was mainly at sea. The flashes continued and the lightening moved behind us as we progressed back to course and Tulsa Riverside airport. We saw the lights of the airport and we talked all the way down to the ground about the strange events that nature can create. We parked the plane and tied the wings down to two rings set in concrete below grass level. It was difficult to find them in the dark, but using a powerful torch out of the window we located the tie down ropes. I dropped the keys on the top of the book case in the office and wrote the time in the book on the counter. Jim and I walked to our vehicles and shook hands as Jim said, 'Night, see you Monday.'

The drive home was one that I had done hundreds of times so I could hardly remember a single road when I arrived home. The low single story sprawling building had lights down the side of the drive and also down the path to the wide double front doors. The front garden was all grass except for some shrubs planted by the walls of the house. There were no fences around the gardens, which I had found strange when I first moved to Tulsa. The reason I had been given was that we all had so much space that we did not need to worry about boundaries.

I pressed the electric door opener and the garage door opened as I drove up the drive. Once inside I stopped the engine and immediately heard a phone ringing. I raced to unlock the inside garage door and try to get to the phone. However, it stopped as I entered the room. It was then that I realised I had not phoned to close my flight plan. This would mean that I was overdue and they would start a search. This always started with a phone call as it was mostly pilots forgetting to close their plan.

I called the FAA number to close the plan and gave them my details.

'Ah Mr Harrison a bit later than your plan. Did

you stop off on the way.'

'No, storms to the south so I just went round,' I said confidently.

'Oh OK, your plan is closed. You can modify the plan from the air you know.'

'Yes, sorry I did not think I would take so long driving back.'

'OK night sir,' he said in a slightly scolding tone.

I put down the phone and felt really annoyed with myself for making such an error. The sort of thing a new pilot does and it was only the second time I had been called to close a plan.

With that I closed the doors and went to bed.

The next day on the news there were all sorts of stories about lights in the sky. I called Jim on the phone, we were vaguely amused that we knew the truth about it. We agreed that we did not want to get involved in any discussions with the press about what we had seen. I certainly did not know enough about the phenomena we saw, to start a public discussion.

As soon as I had put the phone down it rang. I picked it up and I immediately recognised the soft voice of Lorna.

'Hello, Jon?'

'Yes,' I said with surprise.

I said that I was very pleased she had called and asked if she was coming to Tulsa.

'No fraid not.'

'Oh pity,' I said with a disappointed tone.

'Well how about me coming down to McAlester? We could have some lunch,' I said with confidence.

'OK, but make it dinner because I have to work until mid afternoon. Meet me at my house, about six. It will give me a chance to get out of my work clothes and have a shower.'

'OK, see you at six, bye for now,' I said as I put the phone down.

I was so pleased about the call that I called Jim back and told him I would be going down to McAlester this evening to have dinner with Lorna. 'I thought you two would get it together,' he said with a sparkle in his voice. 'I did not plan this Jim!' I said the words, but I had hoped she would call.

'Jon, I am going down that way to visit a friend on Sunday. He is interested in the reports of the unusual storm and we will have a barbecue.'

'OK Jim, have a good time.'

'No! You, have a good time. I'll see you Monday.

Bye.'

Jim was already assuming things that were just the odd idle thought in reality.

I decided to take the van down to McAlester this time, in case I had too much to drink or I decided not to come back until Monday morning.

I showered and sorted through the clothes and selected my favourite shirt, beige cotton trousers and brown plaited leather belt. I also picked up my jeans, a tea shirt, tennis shoes and my wallet and put them in a small bag. I closed the door to the garage and opened the electric door. I climbed into the van and drove out shutting the door with the electronic door closer.

It was a good drive down to McAlester and I arrived at about a quarter to six. She had seen my van arrive and walked down to the gate to join me as I left the van. Lorna looked wonderful in a long, low cut black dress that really showed her beautiful figure. She took my arm and led me up to the house. It was an older house with a few steps up to a veranda. The large double front doors lead into a vast living area with a dark polished wooden floor and carpets between large sofas. A large fireplace was stacked with logs and had a wrought iron screen in front of the range. She showed me around the house and it felt very warm and full of memories.

'I have a surprise for you,' She said with a smile. She opened a large panelled wood door and waved her arm inviting me in. It was the dining room with a long dining room table with a large candle in the middle and the table was laid for two.

'I thought I was taking you out,' I said with surprise. 'Well, I felt like cooking. It's not often, so you need to make the most of it when the urge comes over me.' She pointed at a chair and said, 'Wine?'

'Yes,' I said. 'Red, if you have it.'

She walked to the kitchen and emerged with a bottle of wine. She poured the wine and raised her glass and said

'Welcome to my house.'

'A nice one it is too! It has a really warm feel to it.' She looked at me with a very calm and soft expression.

We had a feast of a meal that she had clearly spent time creating. Rather than courses, it seemed that there was an endless stream of dishes. We then sat in the big sofa and drank coffee. Our conversation went from one thing to the next. She sat at my feet and showed me some photographs. I found it difficult to concentrate on the photographs, with the warmth of her ample breasts resting on my thigh and her perfume that filled the air. All I wanted to do was take her in my arms and kiss her. However, I think she detected that this was the case and she jumped up and said

'More coffee, or would you like something stronger?'

'I'll have a Scotch if you have it?'

'Sure,' she said.

We spent more time talking but, while looking wonderful she was careful not to be so intimate. It is strange but I felt that we both wanted to be closer but were afraid that everything would change.

It was one in the morning and I decided to leave and go back to Tulsa.

'Hey, its late and I have to drive back.'

'OK, I really enjoyed this evening,' She said.

'So did I, dinner was terrific, thanks. It was really a lovely surprise.'

At the door she took my arm and as I turned we kissed. I put my arms around her and she felt so warm. I just wanted to hold her close to me forever. After a few seconds she took a small step backwards and looked into my eyes. A big smile came across her face. She gave me a big hug and peck on the cheek and whispered, 'night,' in my ear.

I walked away and turned to look at her. She was leaning on the wooden rail of the veranda and had a big smile on her face as she said in a real Oklahoma accent.

'Y'all come back soon' and blew me a kiss.

'Drive carefully.'

'OK' I said and waved as I jumped into the van. She was still watching as I drove away.

I was in a dream as I drove home. My mind was going over the evening and wondering what would have happened if I had stayed at the front door or not left when I did. You know, all the thoughts that go through your mind. I got home and went straight to bed and sleep, as it was about three in the morning.

I slept until about 10:00 still with the thoughts of the night before and what might be the future with Lorna. I analysed every comment and still came to the same conclusion, she was definitely interested!

I decided to call her in the afternoon in case she slept longer than me.

To my disappointment the phone rang and did not even have a phone message. I tried to convince myself not expect anything but just call tomorrow. Having done all the distraction jobs, like cleaning the van inside and out by about six in the evening, I watched some TV and finally found myself asleep on the sofa at about ten.

I made tea and took it to bed putting the radio on sleep for about 1 hour.

CHAPTER 2

NOW IT BEGINS.

I woke to the ring of the telephone.

The voice said, 'Mr Harrison?',

'Yes?' I said half asleep.

'This is sergeant Rick Morton Oklahoma state police, we have your friend Jim Garland.'

'Oh, what has he done?'

'I am afraid he is helping us with our enquiries in a murder case,' he said in a solemn voice.

'My god, I cant believe it. Can I talk to him?'

'Yes, hold on.'

I waited what seemed like minutes.

'Hello Jon,' he said in a low tone.

'Hi Jim, What's happened?'

'It's not what it seems. You need to get me some things and a lawyer. I am sorry to drag you into this Jon.'

I said that it was OK and I would take a couple of days off and get things sorted out. I took the address of the police station and the phone number and wrote them down on the telephone pad.

The sergeant was then on the phone again. 'Hello again, this is sergeant Morton. Are you able to appoint someone to represent Mr Garland?'

'Yes, I will arrange everything and bring him some clothes and essentials as soon as I can, maybe two hours.'

'Oh, that's fine.' He said with a lighter voice. 'And your name sir?'

'Oh yes, Jon Harrison.'

'Right sir, we will see you in a couple of hours.'

I spent the next 30 minutes looking for telephone numbers in my book and calling the Company law firm to see who they would recommend to represent Jim. Fortunately they said they would locate the best person they could find and get them to the police station within the next couple of hours. I threw some of my clothes into a bag and made sure I had my washing kit, in case I had to stay down there. This left me with the task of going over to Jim's house and getting some clothes and washing items from his bathroom. It was fortunate that I knew where he left his key. I was still unable to come to terms with the fact that my friend of twenty years had somehow become entangled in a murder.

I drove down the road that was becoming very familiar now. I was now going a little faster than I had last night. In fact I was exceeding the speed limit by a significant amount. I decided that I would not be doing Jim a favour if I was stopped for speeding, so I set the cruise control for sixty miles per hour, as I assumed that the police would not stop me for five over the limit. Due to my racing thoughts of Jim in prison, I hardly remember the road and I seemed to arrive in the town quicker than I expected. The police station was easy to locate by the large fenced car park full of black and white police cars.

I walked up the steps and into a reception area. The officer behind the desk was enormous, at least six foot six inches. He threw me a smile and said, 'Can I help you?' I gave him the information and my contact name, sergeant Morton. I was shown to a room that was bare, with the exception of a table that was screwed to the floor with brackets and four chairs. Sergeant Morton soon arrived.

'Mr Harrison?'

'Yes' I said.

'Take a seat,' he said pointing to a chair. He took the seat the other side of the table. He proceeded to take a note of my relationship to Jim and how long I had known him. He then asked a question that initially through me. 'Did you know Dr Fielding?' It was clear from his question that it was Dr Fielding that had been murdered. From my delay in answering it was obvious that I did.

'Yes, he was one of our customers.'

'I assume it was the Dr that was murdered?'

'Yes, I am afraid so,' he said looking at his notes.

'How well did you know him?' I did not need to think about this question and I answered quickly.

'Oh, I didn't. I just knew he was one of the customers who placed design contracts with us. Jim did the sales of this type of business. I am more involved in the large systems.'

'OK,' he said with a suspicious glance.

The questions went on for some time until I said,

'Can I see Jim?'

'Yes, I think that would be OK.'

He jumped up and picked up a wall mounted telephone and said,

'Bring Mr Garland to room two, Thanks.'

With that he left the room. It was only a few minutes before Jim came into the room, led by another officer. The officer led Jim to a chair and he took the other chair and sat some distance away in the corner of the room. I shook Jim's hand and he sat down.

'How are you,' I said.

'Oh not so bad. I still cant believe that I am here. The police doctor looked at me just now and he said I was fine.'

With that Jim pulled the hair away from above his left eye and I could see a black raised bruise and some broken skin that had clearly been bleeding.

'Someone hit me,' He said with a disgusted expression.

'What in the police station!' I said indignantly looking at the officer. The officer said nothing but shook his head purposefully.

'No! not here, in Fielding's house. I won't go into it at the moment, but I have been framed. All I remember is walking into his front door calling his name and then he met me as I came in the door but did not seem to want me to come in. I guess that's when they hit me. When I woke up sergeant Morton was taking my pulse and kneeling over me.'

Jim explained that they had taken him to the local hospital where, after some tests, they wanted to keep him in overnight just to be safe. Jim had not slept and asked if he could go home. Sergeant Morton arranged hospital transport to the police station and said he could make some calls to his family from there.

Jim was looking very confused and it was clear to me that he had stumbled into something that he did not understand. I had known him for long enough to know that he really did not know how he had become a suspect in a murder.

I saw two men in business suits walking into an adjacent room and it was only a couple of minutes before they came into the room. They were the legal team that had been appointed to represent Jim. We all made our introductions. The older of the two came over to me. He had introduced himself as Paul Grey of Richardson & Grey. He was a man of about sixty but with an aura of power and authority that gave me a feeling of confidence.

'Jim is in good hands, we have had a briefing from sergeant Morton.' He looked over at the police officer with a penetrating stare.

'Have you completed the report?'

The police officer replied, 'Yes Sir we have.'

'Sergeant Morton has got the information and prints.'

The lawyer waited for a second and seeing that he was not going to leave on his own said,

'OK then, may we have some time with our client.' The officer then left the room.

Mr Grey then pulled up a chair and sat at the end of the table. He said that Jim would not be detained, with Jim's unblemished record and the fact he was unarmed, he would be back home soon. He drew a long breath and then said with a low voice.

'Then we start any real work, if required.' He continued to explain the legal process and his concern about the time the case might take. He suddenly stood up and said,

'Lets get Jim home first!'

He walked towards the door, knocked on the glass and the officer came back in the room as Mr Grey and his assistant left.

All Jim could do was sit and stare at his hands. He looked me in the eyes and said.

'I really appreciate all you have done Jon.' I

smiled at him sympathetically.

'We will sort this out.'

'You will be out of here in a couple of hours.'

We talked about the day but were both aware that the officer was observing and listening so avoided the real discussion that we both wanted to have. How had he come to be at Dr Fielding's house.

It was late in the evening before I was driving Jim home in my van. They had kept Jim's car for additional forensic tests. We talked for a while in my van and I told Jim to go in and get some rest and to stay calm, if that was possible. I told him to call me when he was awake in the morning as he had not had a good day today.

In the morning the first thing that came into my mind was that I had not called Lorna, I waited until about 09:00 and gave her a call.

'Lorna, hi I just wanted to call you and let you know why I have not called since I saw you last. My partner in business, Jim has been a guest of the local police as he was found unconscious at the scene of a murder. It was one of our customers.'

'Oh my god, was he alright?'

'Er, sort of, since the man was shot and poor Jim

was unarmed and had a significant bang on the head they let him go. Seems like it may have been a robbery.'

'Oh how terrible, I expect you have been pretty busy getting things sorted out then.'

'Yes, it has been a bit hectic, but I wanted to tell you how much I enjoyed our dinner and maybe get a return date set up.'

'Oh I am sorry Jon, I would love to, but I am not able to do anything for the next week as I am in Washington, but as soon as I am back I will give you a call.'

'OK I'll look forward to that. Have a good trip.'

'I will Jon and you look after yourself and don't do anything that might involve any trouble.'

'OK Lorna, bye for now.'

Lorna sounded a bit stressed in her voice and was very concerned that I should not get involved. Naturally, I suppose, if you were to assume that she had some interest in our possible relationship. I thought to myself that maybe it was my wishful thinking.

It was about lunch time and I thought I would go round to visit Jim, catch up with the latest on the shooting and the impact on either the business or any possible links to Jim himself. Not that I had too many concerns about this, as he was not armed and he was also attacked. I was sure that he would be questioned further, about why he was there and what his relationship was with Dr Fielding.

Jim was at home when I called, so I immediately drove to his house. I parked the Chevy van behind his car in the drive, walked across the well manicured garden and rang the bell. He came to the door with his half frame glasses on his nose, as if he had been studying for some hours. We walked through to his office just off the large living area and down a few steps to a room with a huge desk and filing cabinets on all the other walls. Pictures of Jim getting awards and certificates were on the walls. I had not been to his office many times as we always used our office in town. However, I had the distinct impression that he had emptied the contents of several files on the floor and had many documents open on his desk.

'OK Jon I have been thinking,' he exclaimed, as he sat in his big leather chair.
'I can see that'. I said.

'It looks like you have started some sort of paper trail.'

'Well, I just wanted to do some digging about what exactly Dr Fielding was working on and how it related to what we were making for him, and, well I am a bit concerned that we may be into something more than some new machine tool cutting technology!'

'Hey, steady on Jim, lets not jump to any conclusions. What are you thinking?'

'Jon, we, no sorry let me re-phrase that, I clearly did not do much investigating before undertaking this job.'

'But why would we, we were not expecting anything other than small specialist laser and plasma cutting tools, which is what Dr Fielding has been building for the past few years'. I said in reply.

Jim stared at the floor for some seconds, that seemed like ages.

'Yes, that's what I thought and I did not check for anything more sinister.'

'More sinister!' I exclaimed.

'Yes, Jon, like some sort of weapon!'

'But Jim what small, very small, business would

have the resources to put a multi million dollar weapon project together?'

'What if some foreign power was actually building the project and Dr Fielding was providing the design and parts?'. Jim looked at me with a penetrating stare.

'And, we had made some of the key control elements!' he continued.

'OK, so why would they kill the chief designer?'.

A silence continued for what seemed like minutes.

'All this is speculation right now, isn't it?' I said to break the silence.

'Yes, all we have to go on is our control circuits and the inputs and outputs to the system'. Jim said, pointing to a drawing on the desk.

We talked for about an hour about the design and why Jim thought this might be an advanced new system for controlling very high energy. It seemed to have all the aspects of the control systems required to tune the system to allow for dynamically changing atmospheric conditions over a longer range than the normal few inches. The next question was, who should we talk to about this, if we can get some facts together.

We decided that Jim should do some more work to verify his current thinking and I would investigate our possible future strategy. But until we had some coherent thoughts on what to do, we should not talk to anyone, even the police about our suspicions. We should, continue to respond to their questions and answer factually about our relationship. We had a cup of coffee followed by a Scotch on the rocks and I left late in the evening with my mind in a buzz.

It was 7am next morning when I called Jim to see how he was and to ask if he had slept as little as me.

'Jon, come on over and have some coffee and breakfast and we can compare notes'.

By 8:15 I was back in his office and it seemed that I had never left the night before. The papers were still spread over the office and Jim was still sitting in the same chair. We made coffee and pile of toast and started looking at some of Jim's notes.

'OK Jon, I have the analysis of the project and reasons for my concern'.

He handed me a folder with about 10 pages of text and diagrams.

'Jim, you realize that we are taking some risks

here, digging into the possible plots. Don't forget someone killed Dr Fielding probably because of this knowledge. We may in fact be implicated in whatever, conspiracy materializes.'

Jim shrugged his shoulders and thought for a moment.

'If they had wanted to get rid of me they could have easily done that'. he said, with an air of finality.

From the few hints that the police had dropped, it seemed that they thought it was a normal robbery, as they had taken all the valuable computer equipment. They also thought that maybe Dr Fielding had resisted or even tried to prevent the robbery.

'Art Fielding was sure in a state when I met him at his house for that fateful barbecue. I guess I should have realised that things were not normal when he handed me his business card and tried to say that I should call him at that number some time later. It was just after that someone hit me and I went out like a light.' Jim said, in a low voice and with a puzzled expression.

'Crazy really because I have been dealing with him for about 6 months and have been sending electronic design files to him and phoning him all that time. He must have known that there were people in the house and was trying to get me to leave.'

A thought came into my mind as Jim was talking. It was one of those thoughts that just suddenly materialize. Not a long consideration of all the facts.

'So where is that business card Jim?' I said almost as Jim was still speaking.

'What?' said Jim in a questioning tone.

'The business card that Art gave you as you came in the door.' I continued. 'The one with the phone numbers on it.'

'I don't know. But I'm sure I have another one in my files at the office.'

'Your not getting the point Jim. Art is a very bright and quick thinking man, right.' I explained. 'Why would he hand you information that he knows you already have?'

Jim thought for a moment and then he understood my thought process. I followed Jim up to his bedroom and we went through all the pockets of the clothes he was wearing on the fateful day. Sure enough in the right trouser pocket was the business card. It looked like one that had been used for some time, as the corners were turned over slightly and the card had begun to separate. Apart from that there was nothing special about the front of the card. It just said, Dr A Fielding, Specialist Physics Inc. and the phone and fax numbers of his office and a hand written phone number.

However, on the back were just a string of numbers and letters. Almost seemed random, except that I recognised something about the structure of this string of characters.

Jim and I looked at the card for some time and after a few minutes we almost simultaneously came to the same thought, but Jim just beat me to saying what he had deduced.

'Jon, that's an encryption key. Like the ones we use for gaining access to our protected design files. Except this one is a lot longer!' I nodded and said 'yes, it is the hexadecimal key because all the letters are between a and f.'

As we had both been in software for many years, it was quite common for us to enter values in computer code in hex, as it is called. Hex uses 1 to 9 and then a to f to represent a four bit number up to the decimal value of 0 to 15, that is 16 numbers.

We were both now sure that this was an encryption key and from the length a pretty secure one. The big question is now what is it a key to? Since it is a software key and not just a safe number, then it must be to access something on his computers. Jim and I looked at each other in a despondent way.

'Jim, all his computer equipment in the house was taken wasn't it?' I questioned, just to be sure.

'Yes, all just ripped out from the cabinets and even the keyboards and screens gone.' Jim said in disgust.

We talked for some time and thought that he might just have a duplicate set of computers at his so called 'laboratory'. Really more like a workshop, with some simple machine tools, test equipment and some specialist instruments used in the production of prototypes and proof of concept demonstration systems such as the one we were working on with him.

'Have you been to the lab Jim?' I asked. 'Sure, quite a few times to deliver bits and to have him explain changes,'

'Did you see any computers?' I replied quickly.

'Loads of industrial rack mounted boards and he did mention something about the fastest machine on the nearly public market!'

'Great!' I said with an air of finality. 'All we have

to do is get access to that computer system and we may have a chance to access whatever Art clearly wants us to have.'

It would not be easy to gain access to his system without us being at risk of being seen by the people who killed Art. Jim got out a map and we decided that we would take a flight down to McAlester field and fly over the location of his lab and check the surroundings for potential access. We also discussed calling sergeant Morton to see if there were any developments from his perspective. This could be done under the pretext of us trying to get our business back to normal. Maybe we could ask if we should post outstanding invoices out to his executor and what chance there was of us recovering any of the materials and equipment we had shipped.

Since it was now 14:30 on Thursday we decided to take a rest on Friday and call Rick Morton on Monday and continue with the normal weekend activities like eating out and going down to the golf club as we often did at the weekend. This would hopefully take some of the stress out of the situation. I also decided to call Lorna again and see if she was back from her trip.

CHAPTER 3

I awoke at 8:15 on Friday morning after a night of restless sleep where my brain was trying to second guess the outcome of everything we were planning. I made coffee and sat looking out of the window for all of 5 minutes before I had to start doing something towards next weeks activities. I got out the street map that would have the location of Art Fieldings lab and also the aviation sectional chart for that area. From Jim's exact street location and the description of the property I located the exact spot on the chart and drew a cross. It would be easy to find as there was only one road into this large plot and the building had a large car park for the very small building. No other roads around the building for about half a mile.

I then drew lines to prominent landmarks within a mile of the cross on the chart and measured the angles. This would help identify the exact location when I was flying, but it looked as if it would be easy to spot from about 1500 to 2000 feet.

The phone rang and it was Ann Tomlinson. Ann was the wife of a friend Mark, who often played golf on the weekend. 'Hi Ann, how are you?'

'I am fine, Jon. Just wondered if you wanted to play a round on Saturday?' She said with a devilish tone.

I thought I would join in the little tease and responded, 'OK, your house or mine?'

She laughed and giggled for a while and then I heard Mark in the background say 'Just leave the poor guy alone and ask him if he wants to meet us for lunch and a game of golf.'

'OK Ann,' I said 'If I can't take you up on the first offer, I will make do with lunch and golf.'

She had another giggle and then said to Mark, 'He will join us.'

We agreed to meet at about 12 o'clock Saturday and have a light lunch at the club and then do at least 9 holes of golf.

I first met Mark some years ago when he

was a military adviser on an IBM secret aviation programme. He was not an aviator but he was involved in the security and ground based defensive system. He had all the natural authority and inner confidence of someone who could hold his own in a multi million defence contract. He married Ann when they left University and had two sons that were in their teens. They had many of the obvious signs of wealth in the USA. Two large cars, a big house surrounded by trees with a circular drive with two sets of electric gates and of course the large covered pool at the back that looked like a Roman villa.

I called Jim to see if he was interested in joining us for lunch.

He answered in jolly mood. 'Hi Jon, what's new?'

I was pleased that he had recovered his normal happy personality and seemed back to his normal self.

'Fancy a little lunch with the Tomlinson's followed by golf?'

I said reflecting his happy mood.

'Not this weekend' he said.

'I've been invited to my neighbours 40th birthday and I have to go and find him a suitable present and then go to the party in the evening. I thought what you said about trying to get back to normal, was the right way to go. Give me a call on Sunday, not too early.'

I told him I was glad he was back to his normal self and to have a great time at the party.

I tried Lorna's number but got the same message as last time, so it looked like she had not got back yet, or maybe it was a late flight back from Washington. I was more than a little disappointed.

I showered and got dressed for lunch and golf. The weather was hot, so a long sleeve shirt and some light trousers were the best solution. I also took a straw hat to keep the sun off my head and neck. The golf clubs were in the garage, so I loaded them into the van through the side door and rolled it shut with some force as the door is heavy. I climbed in the front seat and pressed the door opener. As the door rolled up and open I started the engine and watched for the door to be fully open before I drove out of the garage and into the heat. I did not put the air-conditioning on but opened the windows and the breeze was enough to cool me down.

The golf club was out near Riverside airport and has a significant hill overlooking the club where the elite of the IBM community had houses. I have flown over this area many times and each had its own pool and the nearer the top of the hill the larger the houses, except for a few very large properties near the golf course.

I arrived at the club with tennis courts and several very impressive buildings, one of which was the bar and one of two restaurants. Mark and Ann were already there and had a table outside under a large sun shade. Ann gave me a hug and Mark simultaneously shook my hand, which nearly through me off balance.

'What are you drinking Jon?' Mark said in a powerful voice.

'Oh, I'll just have a juice thanks, otherwise you might win!' I said laughing.

This was a real joke because I was still to get an official handicap and Mark had a handicap of 7, which made him about 5 years ahead of me, by my estimation.

Mark got all the drinks and we talked about everything except business. Ranging from the children to the possible investments Mark had been looking at. Ann asked about my current situation in terms of girlfriends.

'Are you still seeing that cute young thing, Emily.' She said raising her eyebrows.

'Oh no, she was a bit too young and well, a bit too different!' I exclaimed. 'You know the short hair and tight jeans.'

'I know what you mean Jon' Ann said with a knowing look.

Emily Jones was a third generation Japanese American very small with short black hair and very pretty. She was also a very good programmer working for IBM and doing some of her own software on the side. She was quite special as she could handle all levels of code from the controller logic arrays to full size mainframe.

The thought went through my mind that there was no question, Lorna would be the one to occupy my life unless it didn't work out.

We spent a couple of hours getting some lunch from the well stocked buffet. I had a spinach salad with a sweet bacon sauce and a selection of cheese and raw vegetables to try and feel fit for a round of golf after lunch.

We finally finished lunch at about 3 pm and the worst of the heat had already gone out of the day.

We picked up our clubs and followed Mark to the golf buggy. Mark put all the clubs in the back and jumped aboard.

We hardly went any distance before the first tee was next to us. Ann went to the ladies tee and drove off.

'You stick with me Jon and we will let Mark wait for us at each hole.' She said as she waved me onto the tee.

My first drive off the tee looked good to start with, but then drifted off to the right. This was to set the trend for the rest of the day. Needless to say I took a lot more shots than Ann and we decided to quit after only 9 holes as we were close to the club house and I had run out of balls.

We said our goodbye's and Mark made a joke about having another game when I stocked up on golf balls.

The drive back home was pretty quiet and I stopped to pick up some beer from a Seven Eleven close to home. Once I had parked the van back in the garage I just sat in the back garden and watched the sun go down and drank a couple of cold beer's. All the events of last week seemed a long way off, but the lack of contact with Lorna was playing on my mind.

CHAPTER 4

I awoke at about 09:45 on Sunday. Very late for me. It must have been the exercise and relaxation from the stress of the previous week. I decided not to call Jim but wait for him to call me in case he had a rather better night than he was expecting. So I went on with the normal chores that often filled Sundays, washing, cleaning and catching up with the routine bills.

Jim eventually called me at about 4pm and did not sound very lively. 'Hi Jon,' he said with a slightly croaky voice.

'Hello Jim sounds like you had a good party last night.'

'Sure did, those neighbours sure live life in the fast lane. I arrived at about 8pm and they were, well on their way.'

'Jon, I am not feeling like much today so I think it is best that I recover and then we meet at the office Monday morning as normal.'

'OK Jim, you take it easy and get an early night. Glad you had a good time.' I said laughing.

'OK Jon thanks, see you tomorrow buddy.'

While I was filling my time with activities, I was building a sequence of events for Monday. This would be, ring Rick Morton on the pretext of trying to sort out what to do next on the project invoices and spare parts. Check on the exact location of Art Fielding's lab with Jim and plan a flight down to look it over from the air and see if anyone is watching it.

Finally call Lorna, she must be back by now, I thought with a feeling like I had been abandoned.

I finally packed my case with the marked up sectional and book of phone numbers.

ΔΔΔ

Our office was a single storey brick building with and entrance on each side as the building was shared by 4 small businesses. Well strictly speaking only three because one was not occupied as they had closed down. The car park had about 6 spaces on each side and our part was on the east side. We had no fancy sign outside just a simple sign with our Company logo and the name H&G Design with contact numbers inside the glass front door.

I got in first and opened to two locks on the door and turned off the alarm system. The office was a simple arrangement with a small entrance room with a corridor running directly away from the entrance with two rooms off to the left and one large room off to the right. The second room on the left had no windows so was used for files and had shelving for parts and electronics assemblies that had been shipped to us..

Each of the offices was glazed on the corridor wall to allow more light. The large room on the right was used as both a meeting room at one end with a folding partition in the middle and a small table and a drawing board at the other end. This was about the smallest business unit that was available in Tulsa, but we had started up the business in a bit of a hurry on the back of being offered a contract, so had almost set it up over night. That was 10 years ago and now we had just about outgrown the space and it was evident from the piles of folders and the fact we had taken half the floor space in the store room with drawings and boxes of equipment.

However, Jim was amazing. I could ask him for a letter or drawing and he would lift up three or four folders and take out the item. He seemed to have a photographic memory for each item.

My desk was in the first office under the window that faced the main entrance to the office block, so I saw Jim as he drove his brown slightly rusting Chevy Malibu into the car park and parked next to my van.

He saw me through the window and lifted his hand in greeting as he walked in the entrance door. He came into the first small office we shared and dropped a pile of folders on his desk the other side of the door.

'Well,' he said with a flourish. 'I guess we had better get started on the Fielding business.'

I explained the thoughts I had on Sunday and how we should call up and try to appear that we are operating, 'business and usual'.

'OK Jon, Rick Morton first then.'

I got his number from a scrap of paper that I had used at the time I picked up Jim from the police. I pressed the buttons on the phone and listened to the dialling tone. Finally I got the station operator and I asked for Sergeant Morton.

' I'm sorry sir he is in a meeting right now, shall I tell him you called.' 'Yes,' I said. 'If you could say it is Jon Harrison just calling about the Dr Fielding case.'

'Thank you sir, I will give him the message as soon as he gets out of the meeting, does he have your number?'

'Yes we are at my office number. He has all our contact information.' I gave him the number just to save Rick Morton time searching his files.

'OK got that sir, thank you for calling.'

I hated sitting around waiting for people to call back or playing telephone tennis because I had not sat and waited for them to call back. But Jim and I decided to use the time to check the flight plan for tomorrow and then I would call Lorna.

We planned a flight that would take us over the Fielding lab and Jim made a note to get some binoculars from home so that if the air was still enough we could maybe take a closer look.

The phone rang and it was Rick Morton.

'Hello Mr Harrison sorry I was not available, what can I do for you?'

'We are trying to get ourselves back to normal

and wondered about who we should talk to now about invoices and shipments, as we are providing equipment for his projects.'

I tried to sound very routine about our business.

'Ah, I see.' He said in an almost relieved voice.

'I guess you have a business to run. I had not really got round to those aspects yet. But since he has no family and it was a one man business, an executor has been assigned to close things up. Let me find the name and number, hold on.'

I could hear the sounds of filing cabinet draws opening and papers being shuffled.

'Yes, here we are. Got a pen?'

'Yes.' I said.

'OK, J & R Dawson of Oklahoma City.' He gave us all the names and contact telephone numbers.

'OK, thanks. Any progress on the case yet.' I said in as casual a way as I could muster.

'Well, I cannot go into that yet, but your friend does not need to worry as it seems they used his visit to attack the Fielding house and he may have just been in the wrong place at the wrong time.' He said quietly.

'Seems like a very professional job from all the evidence so far and they may have been after the cash, in addition to all his expensive computer kit.'

'As soon as we have made some progress I will let you know' He said with an air of finality.

'Anything else I can do for you?'

'No, thanks for the information. We will try to close out the business side. Bye for now and thanks again for calling back.' I said.

He said 'OK, Bye.'

I looked at Jim and said. 'Did you get the basics of that conversation.'

'Yes, I could hear most of it from your handset.' Jim replied.

Jim looked a little puzzled.

'Did I hear him say it looked like a pro job and they were after cash?'

'Yes, that's what he said.' I replied.

'Interesting, I always thought that Art was loaded! So it was not just the computer stuff!' Jim looked at me and raised his eyebrows.

'Jim did you call the number on the business card?' I said, remembering some of the threads of our conversation on Friday.

'Yes I did. But I called from a phone in town, when I was out looking for birthday presents. You know just in case it was being monitored. Not really surprising, there was a computer message saying that no one was available and to call back later.'

'I agree' I said.

'What was that number? Maybe there is something about the number.'

'Jim, have you got the Specialist Physics account file?'

Jim did his usual careful selection from one of the many files that seemed to almost be a random pile on his desk. He handed it to me.

'Lets just check his company phone number.' I said turning the pages.

'Here we are. Where is the business card?'

Jim took the card from his wallet and handed it too me.

I did not even need to read past the first couple of digits, they were both completely different, even the area code.

'Different Jim.' I exclaimed.

'Lets give the number a call again.'

I put the phone on speaker this time and dialled the number.

After two rings a a voice said.

'Hello Jim. I will keep this short. This message is from a remote and hidden computer system that is attached to a phone and recognises only your phone numbers.'

We both looked at each other in amazement. The message continued. Jim whispered. 'It's Art Fielding.'

'You are the only person I can trust now. Please follow these instructions as it is a matter of life and death for a great many people.'

'Only you can access the files on this system. I'm sure you know how. But the site is only active for 5 minutes after each time you make this call. If for some reason the time between calls exceeds a week the computer has a small charge on the drive to destroy the data.'

'The business card has the computer access information along with everything else you need.'

'Jim, I made some mistakes and trusted the wrong people, don't make the same mistake. I thought this was a normal defence funded contract. Only you can put it right. Thanks'

The line went quiet for a moment and then a tone came on the line like a modem. I waited for a while and then put the phone down.

We sat and looked at each other in stunned amazement.

The words, life and death for a great many people, sent a chill down my spine.

'Jim, what the hell was he...'

I stopped mid sentence.

'Jim, what were, <u>we</u> building.'

Jim looked at the floor and eventually looked up with his fingers interlocked and leaning on his knees.

'I said I had my fears, I think we now know.'

Jim went very quiet.

'OK.' I said abruptly, to snap us both out of this state of mind.

'We need to get the information that Art felt was so critical and be sure it gets into the right hands.'

I thought for a moment. How many people could I really trust with life and death information that is clearly of national importance. I bet I can count them on one hand.

My thoughts then drifted to Lorna and why it had been three days since we had been in contact. Maybe I was reading more into our last meeting than she was.

'Jim, I'm just going to call Lorna.'

'OK, I will just go and file this pile next door.' He said with just a hint of a smile.

I found the number in my phone book and dialled. The phone now just rang and did not even go on to the answer phone. I felt more than a little deflated by this result. But, what did it mean.

Jim then came back and could see from my expression that she had not been there.

'Hey Jon, I'll call that number for the executor.'

'OK Jim, I'm just going for a quick walk around the block to get some air.' I said getting up from my chair.

On my walk around the building I thought about the possible reasons for Lorna not responding. Maybe she had been kept in Washington in meetings. I decided that when we flew down to look at the fielding lab, I could call in to see if she was back.

When I got back to my desk Jim had made the call and he explained that the guy handling the case had only just been assigned but would need about a week to do the necessary searches on family, banks and the business aspects.

'OK, Jim we were maybe a little quick off the mark there, but we should keep in touch.'

'Are we ready for the trip down to the lab later or tomorrow?'

I had not done any more than decide to fly down and also to visit Lorna. We had not really thought through what we would be looking for other than the computers that would would be accessed by the encryption key on the business card. The call to the phone number and the message from Art had sort of changed all that.

'It would be interesting to know what is in the building but we don't have access Jim.'

'Ah well, if we find that there is no one around I have the combination and the alarm code in the file as I have personally taken circuit boards and interface information down there several times over the past six months.'

'Wow, he really did trust you then.' I said with a little surprise.

'Yes, but he was a hard person to get close to and I never felt like he was a close friend. But trusted, yes.'

We talked for a while about the trip and how we could try to keep it low profile. I proposed that it could be just going to visit Lorna but we could look over the place and see if it was obviously being watched by anyone. Jim agreed and we made all the necessary calls to the Riverside flying club and booked the same Cessna 172 that we rented last time. Jim made a mental note to take his binoculars.

We would go mid afternoon tomorrow and hope the turbulence was not too great by the time we got to McAlester so we could see the lab and also Lorna's house.

The airport was very quiet as usual with only the odd student doing some local flying and learning the skills of landing. This was accomplished by just touching the wheels on the runway and then raising the flaps to 10 degrees, putting the power on and climbing out to do another approach. We picked up the keys and as usual I did the walk around the plane and checked fuel and tyres. The young boy was not around this time but the planes were always ready for customers and often parked at the fuel pumps ready to go.

The air traffic was very quiet and I got clearance for a south departure and immediate take-off, after I had done some engine checks and while I was still rolling towards the runway.

After we flew over the lakes that were close to McAlester, we prepared our course and used some landmarks to line ourselves up to pass just to the left of the lab. Jim started a mile by mile detailed commentary of ground features and gave instructions like, 'maybe a little to the right.' This was in order to correct the course, so that he could get the best view through the binoculars.

The count down continued and I reduced altitude down to about 1500 feet and reduced power to slow down as much as possible. 'Five miles now Jon. I think I can see the road and....My God! the building has gone.'

'Are you sure?' I said reducing power more and starting a turn to give Jim the best view.

It was very clear that the building had been completely destroyed and all that was left were neat piles of debris. We looked around for cars or even people walking around the area or on the single access road. 'Not a soul in sight,' Jim said after our third circle round the site.

'OK, not much point in looking around the burnt out site, lets go and look up Lorna.' We headed towards the airport but before I could call on the radio Jim said, 'I'm not sure that's a good idea, I can see Lorna's house and she has visitors.' 'Two black cars next to hers out the front.' Jim was looking through the binoculars and avoiding the wing struts by leaning forward.

I made an instant decision not to land and to fly back as I did not want to barge into a business meeting. I just thought with two black company cars at her house, maybe she was really busy and had set up a meeting at her house. At least I knew she was back from her business trip and I should be able to call her later.

We headed back to Tulsa and filed a return flight from the air. I took the opportunity to be able to talk to Jim on the intercom without any risk of anyone overhearing. 'Jim, this is really coming down to who we can trust with this sensitive information. You know how Art felt about this.' 'I sure do, but I think this gives us a problem.' he said with a sigh of desperation.

'Well maybe not, I have an idea.'

I proceeded to explain an idea I had been going over since we had the message from Art. It was clear to me that we did not have anyone within the defence or security community that we knew well enough to just hand Art's secrets over. There were some people that we had absolute trust in and they were in the right place to possibly have trusted contacts of their own.

There was also a very trusted ex-girlfriend who has all the skills we need when it comes to the internet and software.

After some discussion about the detail Jim said, 'Seems like a plan to me!'

'The only concern I have Jim, is that we must take care to make sure they do not become targets themselves.'

'Tricky one,' Jim replied.

We landed at Tulsa Riverside and went our separate ways. Jim was going home to try and resume some work on some of the smaller projects before the weekend. I would use the payphone at the airport to call Mark Tomlinson and set up a game of golf.

I have known Mark for years and his wife before that. Anyone seeing this if they were interested would not see this as anything unusual. Mark has a security clearance that as he said once, 'If you knew the level of my clearance I'd have to shoot you!'

The next step would be to visit a bar that Emily has been going to for years.

Emily and I were very close, in fact we lived together for about nine months when I first got the business started. The big problem was the fifteen year age gap and we drifted into different life styles. But I still miss her trusting and happy outlook, but she never got out of her dress style, black leather and short black hair which came to points just at her jaw line.

'Mark,' I said as he picked up the phone. 'it's Jon Harrison.'

'Jon great to hear from you, how's the golf ball stock.' He said with a laugh.

'Well that's exactly why I called. Would you like to just do a quick nine holes in the evening this week, followed by a beer.'

'Well, we will start with nine and see how you go. How about Thursday at about 16:00.'

'That's great Mark, give my love to Ann and the boys.' I said.

I wanted to get Mark on his own so I was trying to keep the call short and casual. Of course Mark had known me for years and came back pretty quick.

'Everything all-right with you Jon?' He said with a real questioning voice.

'Sure fine. Might just want to get your ideas on a project or two.' I said casually.

'Oh OK, I look forward to it. See you Saturday.'

That was step one of the plan out of the way and I don't think there was much chance of this being of risk to Mark. Now home and get ready to make an appearance at the bar where Emily would spend an hour after work most days.

I was well aware of the urgency of getting access to the data and getting it into safe hands as soon as possible. I would need to make another call to the number on the business card Monday if I could not get Emily to retrieve the data from the remote site before then.

I had quite a time before six o'clock, when she might be at the bar. I spent some time sitting in the van at the airport and going over what I would say to Emily. The best plan would be to approach her saying I need some help with a serious problem. I would then need to get her on her own and quickly run through recent events.

I arrived at the bar at about six-thirty. I had judged that she would be there for at least a couple of hours and I did not want to stay long if she had decided to depart from her habit of some years. I parked about 200 yards down the street and walked across the busy street and into entrance of the much darker bar.

My eyes took time to adjust to the dim light, but almost immediately I spotted Emily leaning on the corner of the bar with some people I recognised but did not really know. I walked up to the centre of the bar and ordered a beer. It was very busy but she saw me as I leaned over to pick up my beer. I smiled and waved. She walked over and threw her arms round my neck and gave me a kiss, as if we were still together.

'Jon, it's so nice to see you,' she said with her broad smile.

'I'm pleased to see you to,'

'You miss me as much as I miss you?' she said in a solemn tone.

I decided to jump right in and tell her why I was there now.

'Look, I need someone I can trust, and yes I do miss you, but that's not why I am here.' I said in a very soft and serious tone. She tightened her grip round my neck and whispered in my ear, 'You know you can trust me, we know each other so well. What do you need if it's not my body?' she said very softly.

Emily was never shy about saying what she felt or wanted, but this time I think she knew this was more business than intimacy.

'I need to tell you very quickly the events of the last couple of weeks, and it has to be where we can't be overheard.'

'I know just the place, let me just tell my work friends that I need to talk to you for a while.'

She walked back to her friends and just said

a few words and returned with that really lovely smile. She took my hand and led me over to an enclosed booth with a table a four chairs.

'No one can hear us in this corner Jon.'

'Just a quick explanation and then if you can use your skills to retrieve some data for us.' I said in a low voice.

I proceeded to tell the basic story of how Jim and I had got involved in this clearly very dangerous project. I also explained the way in which Dr Art Fielding had constructed a system to protect key design information from falling into the wrong hands.

'I'm in Jon, no problem. Just tell me the precise time you will make the call and unlock the system and I will retrieve the data and put it in whatever form you need to get it in safe hands.'

'How about a digital tape, that is probably the safest and quite small.'

'That's no problem I have loads of them.' she said still in a low voice and whispering in my ear.

'I have a copy of the information and encryption key that was on the business card given to Jim, how about ten in the morning tomorrow? Jim can make the call from the office, it has to be that phone. I will come over to your place at about

09:45 and then take the tape back with me.'

'What will you do with the information?' She said with concern in her voice. 'Don't you think the people who killed Dr Fielding will want to get their hands on it?'

'I do, but they obviously think they have all the data when they took all his computers.' As I said this the thought struck me that they would also have their experts looking through the computers and realise at some point that it was missing or did not work.

'I'll let you get back to your friends. Look after this piece of paper.' I folded the paper into a small square and carefully put it in her hand, out of sight.

'I have to go.' I whispered in her ear.

She put her arms around me and kissed me again. This time I just could not resist. This is what I missed, her passion and fire. I had begun to forget these feelings but they came back with a rush. I found it really hard to leave.

'Jon, see you tomorrow. I won't let you go so easy tomorrow!' She said with some determination.

She blew me a kiss as I walked through the bar to the door. I was feeling quite confused about my feelings for Emily and also Lorna. This occupied me on my drive firstly to Jim's house, to let him know what we needed to do tomorrow, then home to bed.

CHAPTER 5

My alarm seemed extra loud and I fumbled around my bedside table to press the silent button, but first found my watch and an empty glass before hitting the button. The time was 08:30 and within five minutes the phone rang.

'It's Jim, I'm at the office,' he said, but I could tell there was more to the phone call.

'The office is a wreck and all the computers, backup tapes have all gone. The local police are here as they turned up when the alarm went off. They will make a report for our insurance purposes.'

'Don't worry Jim just stay and do what you can and keep our appointment, remember?' I said in a slow and very purposeful manner.

'I will buddy, precisely on time, don't worry. Good luck! Talk later.'

Jim had got the message and also thought of the need for time synchronisation, which I had not thought of. We now knew that they were getting more desperate to get their hands on the information. There was just time for me to shower and dress to drive over to Emily's house. I knew the route to her red brick 1930s three story town house near the centre of Tulsa. Since I knew her she had always owned the top flat and had even kept it when she moved in with me, nearly two years ago.

I parked in the street and went to the entry door and pressed the button with the name E Jones next to it. Her voice came on the intercom.

'Come on up Jon.' The door lock buzzed and I opened the front door.

I went up to the top floor and she greeted me with open arms and a kiss just like she always did. She looked very different to her normal tight jeans and leather jacket look. She wore a brightly coloured flowery halter dress that really showed off how very slim and pretty she was.

'I'm ready with with all the computers up and running. I also have all the likely encryption tools, in case we have any problems. It should just be a case of downloading the data. You go and make some coffee and I will start as soon as it gets to 1 minute past 10:00.' She said as she pointed to her study that resembled a space centre with two rows of three screens. I had seen her work at one of these work centres, as she called them. One set for editing and making changes, the other set of screens for watching the live systems. There was a cable duct coming down the wall in one side of the room to a cabinet in the corner with a smoked glass door and behind the glass a rack of modular systems with what seemed like hundreds of tiny flashing lights. There was also a small glass case screwed to the wall with a sign hanging on it saying, 'DON'T EVEN BREATHE ON THIS!' I knew this was some sort of encryption device for some of her more sensitive work. Apart from the technical equipment the room was large and comfortable with reclining chairs and a large coffee table. There was also a stereo system that had a display screen that I remember seeing her adjust the output from the speakers located in the corners of the room. 'Em' as I used to call her was certainly technically very accomplished, but you would never know it to see her walking down the street.

I made coffee and by the time I had brought it back and put it on the coffee table she had the remote computer on the screen and was reading the instructions. She found the page to answer some questions and to enter a password.

'Password!' She said.

'What password?'

I jumped up and grabbed the copy of the business card printed on the sheet. It was true there did not seem to be a password. I scanned the printed sheet for a clue.

'Try the phone number!' I said.

'No, I think I have it! See that,' She pointed, 'under the company name he has put the word physics in quotes.'

She typed and exclaimed, 'Yes!'

A new page appeared on the screen with lists of files. Emily began loading these onto the tape drive. The light on the small desk tape unit flashed and Emily walked to the coffee table, picked up her coffee and stood in front of the screens, watching the progress of the downloading process. She peered at one screen then the other looking at some monitoring software she was running on the left screen that seemed to be comparing the file sizes with the files listed, and the progress and speed of download on the other.

It was at least 30 minutes before she turned and said, 'Nearly there.'

'Hey the suspense is killing Em,' I said still standing behind her watching the screens.

'We still need to see if the de-cryption is OK though.' She said in calm voice.

'OK finished download, lets decrypt one file just to see.'

The right hand screen then displayed a new page saying in bold print.

'IF YOU ARE SURE YOU HAVE <u>ALL</u> THE DATA REPLY YES.'

Em looked at the log file and compared the file list but turned and looked at me.

'We should decrypt before we say yes, I think. Here goes!'

She ran one software executable file that was downloaded which immediately requested a key. She typed the hexadecimal number from the card. New files were now appearing on the drive and with easily readable titles compared with the numbered files in the list. From my limited experience of file types, I could see drawing files, documents and software source code.

'Smart cookie this Art. He even wrote the software to check it's all there!' She said with some surprise.

A message came up on the screen doing the decryption to say, 'All files correct and checked!'

'OK Jon we are done! Shall I say yes to the message?'

We both looked at each other.

'How sure are we that they are all intact?'

'Look Jon, I have opened this document and this is source code. They are both quite readable and seem to make sense. I think the program that Art wrote to check the completeness of the files was also a good check.' She said with some confidence.

'OK lets answer yes then!' I replied.

Em typed 'YES' into the reply box on the screen and we both stared as the new page came up. It said:

'Thank you Jim, take great care. Self destruct in 10 seconds!'

The page then refreshed with a new blank page. We both stood in silence for a minute and looked at the blank screen. I think we both felt the sort of finality that we knew Art had gone and that he had entrusted Jim to make everything right. The smile had gone from Emily's face and she looked very sad. She sat in the chair opposite me and stared at me.

'What now Jon?'

'I will make sure it gets into the right hands. I have already set that up.' I said reassuringly. ' I must phone Jim at the office and give him the all clear to go home.'

'Here use this phone.' She handed me a phone from the coffee table and I phoned the office number.

'Hi Jim all OK your end?'

'Jon, sure, how about you?'

'Yes, everything is great and working as we planned. But you take care I will call you first thing tomorrow.'

'OK buddy everything is at least tidy and secure here, so I'm off home. See you tomorrow.'

We spent an hour or so looking through the documents many of which were marked 'SECRET' or 'TOP SECRET'. Emily had a clearance at that level but as with everything classified to this level it was all on a 'need to know' basis. Many of the computer aided design files were in a special format and only Jim or the subcontractors that undertook production would be able to read these files on the system that we have, or should I say had at the office.

Em got up from her chair and came over to my chair and sat on my lap with her head on my shoulder. She then put her arms round my neck and gave me a kiss.

'Now that we have all the data stored safely we can relax,' She said in a soft voice close to my ear. She gave me another kiss and it brought back the feelings that I had when we first met and moved into her apartment together.

'I've missed you Jon and I can tell you have missed me.'

She sat upright and reached behind her neck and pulled a bow at her waist at the same time. Her dress slipped to the floor and she put her arms back round my neck. Her beautiful body now looked wonderful as she stood up completely naked and took me by the hand and into the bedroom. As I lay on the bed and she knelt over me I said.

'Should we...'

But she stopped me saying more and kissed me again whispering in my ear.

'I know what we both need right now!'

She had not forgotten anything from our time together and all the things that would excite and give us both pleasure were pursued relentlessly.

I woke with her in my arms. Slowly small movements and contented sounds let me know she was awake and making the most of her time with me. The sun was shining through the open window and I could hear the traffic outside. The reality of the situation with the data for the weapon system and the need to get it into the right hands came to the front of my mind and with that a sense of urgency. I looked around the room and saw the alarm clock.

'Twelve fifty five!' I said reading it again in disbelief.

'Oh Jon you've just arrived back on earth. What a pity I could have stayed like that with you all week.'

She sat up and stretched her arms up in the air then put them round my neck kissed me.

'I have two urgent needs,' I said in a forceful voice as I got up.

'The second one is coffee!' I said as I walked to the bathroom.

'I'm on it! Instant is all I have since you left.'

The main living area of the apartment was very large by city standards. It had two sofas, each one could seat 4 people with ease. The wooden floor had a large Persian style carpet between the two sofas and a low oak coffee table between them. In keeping with the style which Em had adopted it was a very minimalist space.

We sat in one of the sofas and drank coffee and I explained how I planned to hand over the data to Mark. Em had heard his name in IBM on a project she had worked on.

'Ex military I think,' she said in an approving voice.

'I heard he was considered a really tough cookie in the past. He came back from wherever he was with a heap of medals,' she said dramatically.

'Mind you that's just office chatter. But some of his unit are living in town I heard.'

'I think he would be a good person to help you find a home for your disk,' She said finally.

We showered and dressed as if we were still living together. Em sitting in the chair by the window drying her hair and doing her make-up. She put on a pair of tight jeans, a white shirt and leather jacket.

'I need to go to work today but timing is not critical,' She explained.

She looked immaculate and in contrast I looked like I had been sleeping in my clothes, which was far from the truth.

It was now nearly two o'clock and that left me just enough time to get home and change for the game of golf with Mark.

Em gave me a hug as I left and put a small metal case just big enough for the drive into my hand. I gave her a kiss and turned to leave. Just then she grabbed my arm and said.

'Can you come over again soon?'

I turned and smiled.

'Your very special Em.'

I waved to her as I walked over to the van.

I called Jim on his mobile to get him to come over to the golf club at 16:00.

'Hi Jon where have you been? I went round to your house last night. I bet you were paying Lorna a visit,' He said with quiet voice as if it were a secret.

'No, not at Lorna's house, but I will fill you in with the latest at the golf club.'

'Ok, What time?'
'I will be there at 16:00 with Mark.'
'Ok see you in the car park.'

CHAPTER 6

I drove into the car park at the golf club. There were very few cars so it was easy to spot Mark with his elbow out of the window of his Nissan 4X4. Mark's Nissan was a 4 door with a rear door and loads of space in the back.

As I opened my car door he got out and opened the back to take out his clubs and shoes. We sat on the low wall outside the club house and put on our golf shoes.

'Well Jon what's this really about?'

I explained the business with Dr Fielding and how we thought we were making a new cutting machine and about the strange death of the Dr and our initial investigation. How we looked at the design and decided it was a weapon system.

'How sure are you,' He looked at me with a serious expression.

'Oh completely now, I have not finished the story!'

I explained the rest of the situation and how Em had made a tape. I could see that Mark was getting very nervous.

'Jon, where is the tape?'

'In the pocket of my golf bag.'

'OK, I will make some phone calls,' He said looking very serious.

'If this is what I think it is, then the group that killed Fielding will be after you next. As soon as they realise that the kit they stole from your office and Fielding's lab was just a set of empty boxes, the only people left are you and Jim.'

'Jim is on his way over here right now.'

With that information Mark went to his car opened the back and took out his golf clubs. I thought this was strange until I saw him reach deep into the back and take something out. It was a large pistol which he examined carefully and put behind his back. He then reached in the back again for a metal box containing clips of ammunition.

'Mark do you think it will get that serious?'

'Oh yes! These people will stop at nothing to

get the information you have.'

With that Mark got in his car and made some calls on a radio, that he clearly did not want me to hear, as he spoke in a low voice with the handset close to his mouth. He then slid a large metal box from the back of his car so he could open it. I walked over to his car and watched as he opened the metal box. It contained enough weapons for a small war. Rifle, some sort of grenades or explosives but not the normal round ones. He pulled out a small hand gun and loaded it. I watched as he set the safety catch and then he handed it to me.

'You can shoot can't you. We have been to the gun club I think.'

'Yes we went for the barbecue and you had me shooting at the targets.'

'Oh that's right. Pretty good too if I remember. This is the safety,' he said pointing at a small lever on the side of the gun.

'Don't take it out of your pocket unless you mean to use it!' he said with an air of authority.

Mark had now switched from a calm and gentle friend to a primed machine in combat mode. He put his golf clubs in the back of the car, then carefully put mine next to them. He opened the pocket in my golf bag to examine the metal box containing the tape.

'Oh very good,' he said as he placed it back in the pocket.

'That will stand almost anything but a nuclear attack. Where did you get it?'

'Emily the software wizard!'

'Ah, the famous Emily. How is she?'

'She was just great when I left her this morning.'

'You know she is not just a great looker but the best at almost anything technical,' Mark said in a low voice.

'I know. She has worked with your team before.'

Mark looked down the long drive to the club and clearly saw something. It was Jim's car. Mark knew Jim as we had all played golf in the past.

'That's Jim,' I said as the car became more recognisable.

At that moment a black pick-up that was parked at the side of the drive pulled in front of Jim's car. The passenger in the pick-up jumped out and ran and opened Jim's door. At the same instant Mark took the three paces to the back of his car and took out the rifle and a clip of ammunition. Like a machine he inserted the clip and using the bolt, chambered a round and removed the covers on the sight. With his back against the car he looked through the sight, made a couple of clicks of the adjustments on the sight. In this time the man had pulled Jim from the car and was walking towards the pick-up that had driven round Jim's car ready for a quick getaway. The pick-up was parallel to Jim's car. With his back to us and his left arm pushing Jim and what looked like a gun in his right. Mark still did not fire until the man stretched out to open the pick-up rear door. The rifle crack was probably not heard by the man, who was hit in the right arm and spun round falling backwards. Jim took this opportunity to dive in the ditch near the pick-up. Mark looked away from the sight and blinked, simultaneously moving the bolt to chamber the next round. The expelled cartridge case jingled as it hit the tarmac of the car park.

The pick-up driver then got out and went towards Jim, crouching low trying to get cover from the back of the pick-up. Jim was some distance behind the pick-up and as he reached Jim, Mark fired again this time hitting his leg as he came from behind the pick-up. He then fell next to the pick-up and opened the drivers door and pulled himself in. The other man had gained his feet and just managed to get into the passenger door. The pick-up then drove or should I say skidded down the drive and disappeared from sight.

Mark immediately made the rifle safe and replaced the sight covers placed on the back seat. Then said, 'Jump in Jon.' He moved quickly into the driving seat and started the engine. As soon as I had got in the passenger door the tires screeched as we took off at speed towards Jim.

'Looks like you winged both of those guy's' I said quietly.

'That's the idea. That should give their organisation some problems getting them fixed up.'

We arrived at Jim's location in the ditch and he carefully looked up.

'Hi guy's, you finished destroying the opposition?' He said in a triumphant tone.

'You OK Jim.' I said as I jumped out and gave him a concerned look over.

'I am fine, I guess we had better get back to the car park. I will see you there.'

He casually got in the ageing Chevy Malibu and

followed us back to the car park. We all got out and Mark proceeded to pack his rifle, ammunition and lock the steel box back in its position out of view.

'Let's take these golf shoes off, I don't think we will be needing them today. We can then go to the club bar and have a drink. I bet you need one Jim.' Mark pointed to the door at the front of the golf club main building with very short and tidy lawns and flower borders.

'Good idea.' Jim said.

We put our shoes in the back of Marks Nissan and he locked the cover. As we walked in the main door of the club, Mark was greeted by one of the members.

'Hi Mark, you been shooting the critters again?'

'Yes Pete, couple of rabbits that won't be digging holes in our greens!' Mark laughed and we joined in.

We all looked at each other and Mark winked.

'Let's sit round the corner here out of earshot of the others.' He said with a whisper.

'OK, what would you all like to drink?' Mark gestured towards the bar.

'Large scotch for me.' Jim said.

I decided to just have a draft beer. Mark walked

over to the bar and shook hands with a couple of the people at the bar. The barman soon placed a tray of drinks on the bar and Mark returned to the table.

'Scotch for you Jim, Beer Jon and an orange juice and lemonade for me. I might need to shoot some more rabbits before the day is out.' He said with a knowing glance.

'Well, I guess things have really got pretty serious now. We should review what actions we need to take next.' Mark said in a low voice.

'My 'boss' has given me the go ahead to take care of it quietly with <u>no</u> collateral damage. In other words no outside individuals. Nice and clean and tidy, as he put it. Intel seems to indicate some government rogue elements may be involved. He will take care of that end. Who else knows about the tape apart from my team and you two?'

'It is just Em and that is it! You think of anyone else Jim?' I added after some thought.

'No that's it, I am sure.' Jim replied with confidence.

'Did the two guy's say anything while they opened your car door?' Mark questioned as he looked at Jim.

'Let me think. Yes, he said, come with us we

would like your help to collect the data tape to finish our project. Or something like that.'

'Did he say the word <u>tape</u> Jim?' Mark looked at Jim with an urgent expression.

'Er...Yes he did.'

With that response Mark left the table and went to a phone just round the corner from our table. I heard him dial, wait a while and then put the phone down.

'We have no time to waste here, Emily was the only person they could have got that information from and she is not answering her phone. We will go in my car.'

The journey over to Emily's house was as fast as Mark could drive without attracting too much attention. When we arrived at the house, I jumped out and Mark was right behind me watching the street for any possible attack. I pressed the call button next to E Jones. No response. I then pressed the call button for the apartment below E Jones. There was a click and then a lot of rustling followed by a very frail. 'Who is it?'

'I am a friend of Emily Jones, Jon Harrison. I am concerned she not answering her phone or door.'

'Oh hello, she must be so pleased to have so

many friends. I let the other two gentlemen in this morning. Perhaps she has not heard the buzzer, I sometimes miss it. I will let you in and you can knock on her door.'

With that the door buzzed and I opened it. Mark and I entered and ran up the stairs.

As soon as we got to her door my heart sank as we could see fragments of wood on the floor and the door was open about half an inch. Mark pulled his gun and opened the door, quickly moving me aside with one hand. Once inside he made a rapid search of the rooms and found a note in one inch high capital letters. 'We will be in touch Mr Harrison.'

Mark and I looked at each other and I felt a sick feeling in my stomach, as I thought of Emily and how frightened she must be.

'We will get her back Jon. She clearly just said that she made a tape and gave it to you. She will be fine and used as a hostage to get the tape.' Mark said as he put his hands on my shoulders. Mark closed the door with a bit of force and picked up the splintered wood so that it was not obvious that it had been forced. Mark and I headed down the stairs and out of the front door. An older woman in her 80s was leaning on her open window. We waved at her and Mark said. 'She must have gone out with her friends, thanks.'

The lady waved and shut the window.

Mark dropped the splinters of wood in the curb and went across the road to the car. When we got back in the car Mark said in a low voice. 'They got Emily Jim.'

Jim was silent for a minute as he realised the situation.

'I am sorry to hear that Jon, I am sure we can do something. Even give them the damn tape!'

Mark drove to the IBM car park and said he would be about 15 minutes while the tape was copied. He went to the back of the car and got the tape, walked to the gate. He swiped his pass in the reader and the revolving gate allowed him through. When he came back he gave the tape to me and he started the engine.

'I think we should all go to your house Jon and wait for them to contact us. We will go back via the golf club to pick up the cars.'

It was about 45 minutes later that we all arrived at my house and I arranged that Marks Nissan was in the garage where we could access it from inside the house. Just in case we have unexpected and unwanted visitors.

We sat and drank coffee and discussed the options of how to get Emily back. It seemed that they had all the cards, because we did not know where they had Emily or where the system they were building was located. Mark agreed that we were not in control but to make things more even we had to find out where the tape goes when they ask for it. I need to set up my team to track it when it leaves here.

He went to his car and got a radio. It was clearly a portable with a handset so that you could use it as a phone. He placed it in the bay window in the dining room at the front of the house and picked up the handset.

'Alpha one signal check.'

A very noisy signal came from the speaker which Mark turned off. He then moved the radio and signalled to us with a thumbs up. Mark then shut the door to the dining room as he set up his team to track the tape.

I was confident that Mark would not put Emily at risk but was also aware that he had a responsibility to shut down this potential risk to national security.

It was a quarter past four when the phone rang. I jumped up and went to the phone. Mark also jumped up and when I lifted the handset he put his ear close to the handset.

'Mr Harrison?' Said the voice with a slight accent.

'Yes I am Jon Harrison.' I replied.

'OK, Listen carefully. I will send a taxi to pick up the tape from your house tomorrow morning at 09:00. We will be watching to ensure no one follows the taxi. Please do not talk to anyone about this tape or your conversation with us. Please do not involve your trigger happy golfing friend, we were not wishing to make this situation any more complicated than is necessary. Miss Jones will return as soon as we have verified the design is complete. Do you understand?'

'Yes, I understand. I will give the tape to the cab driver. All we want now is to get Emily home.'

With that, the phone went dead.

Mark nodded in approval and seemed to have a renewed energy and enthusiasm in knowing the next steps.

'Mark, I really don't want Emily put at risk by your guy's following the taxi.' I said.

'Jon, I have had years of experience of extracting important people from difficult situations. I will not risk Emily. My team have worked with me for years and have resources and anonymity on their side. They certainly will not just jump in a car and follow the taxi. Don't worry.'

'OK.'

My concern was for poor Emily, who had been so willing to help me and I had caused her to get in this situation that I would do anything to get her out of.

Mark spent some time talking to his team and let them know the time the cab was due to arrive. I then got Jim established in the bedroom next to mine and Mark decided to sleep in the dining room near the radio, on the sofa, so I made him comfortable with pillows and blankets.

I finally went to bed about 01:15 and set my alarm for 08:00, but did not sleep for some time, thinking about Emily and what I would give to turn back time.

CHAPTER 7

The alarm went off and I reached over and hit the button to stop the beeping sound. I could hear movement in the kitchen as coffee was being made and the fridge door was opening with that annoying creak that I always intended to fix. Reality hit me once again and Emily came into my mind and I took a deep intake of breath and leapt out of bed.

I made my way to the kitchen and there were Jim and Mark dressed with coffee and toast.

'We are all ready to go.' Jim said with enthusiasm.

The one thing I really treasure about my friend, is that he can turn a dire situation into a bearable one with just a look or a few words. I must say I needed some enthusiasm this morning. It was 08:25 and Mark had the tape on the table. He looked at me reassuringly.

'It is all set up Jon. We will track the cab from the air. Alpha 2 is a pilot and he is up with a spotter flying a little away from the area right now. He flew in from Stillwater this morning so as not to attract attention. We also have a couple of ground units on highways south and north.'

'OK I think some strong coffee is what I need then.' I said as I walked towards the coffee jug that I know Jim always filled to the top whenever he was at my house for breakfast.

'Did you get any sleep on the sofa Mark?'

'Sure when my guy's stopped chatting. They love some action and they were going through every detail with timing down to the second. I had to calm them down in the end and tell them that I just needed short reports. There is a cable running across the dining room so don't trip. I realised last night I needed to charge the radio and the wall outlet near the radio was switched by the light switch. I did not want to leave the lights on all night.'

At about five minutes to nine Mark and I went to the front door and he stood out of sight while I stood in the open doorway waiting for the cab. It arrived spot on nine o'clock. The driver got out of the white cab with taxi plates and a sign on the side saying, 'Airport Cabs' and the phone number. There were no passengers. I went to walk out to the driver and Mark caught my sleeve to stop me and whispered, 'Let him come up the path to you.'

I moved out of the doorway and waved to the driver who jogged up the driveway.

'You Mr Harrison?'

'Yes, are you picking up this tape? Do you know where you are taking it?'

'Oh I don't know that yet sir. I have to wait for the instructions from the office.'

'OK, here it is, thanks.'

The driver walked away and I went back to the house as he drove off. Mark was already on the radio to Alpha 2 in the air and they clearly had the cab in sight and a good identification of the specific cab.

'Nice try Jon.' Mark said as he put down the handset. You didn't think they would tell the driver anything did you?'

'No but you never know.'

The radio made a beep and Mark picked up the

handset.

'OK, tracking west towards Tulsa International. Alpha 1 out.' Mark replied on the radio.

'Looks like all is going well at the moment.' Mark said as he walked back in the room.

Mark heard the radio again and turned on the speaker this time.

'Alpha 2, He has stopped for gas.'

'Can you see the car.' Mark replied.

'Yes, just the back, he is at one of the pumps.'

Mark looked a little worried. Another voice came on the radio.

'Alpha 3, I'm about a half a mile from the gas station and moving towards target.'

Mark said nothing but listened intently to the radio.

'Alpha 3, He is just pulling out of the gas station, following.'

Mark picked up the handset. 'Alpha 3 keep your distance.'

'Alpha 3, OK boss.'

Mark turned to us. 'There was not enough time for the driver to meet someone.'

For some time the conversation between Alpha 2 and 3 was just about which way the cab had turned and how many cars ahead he was.

'Alpha 2, cab pulled into car park with about 5 other cabs. Driver out and leaning on car.'

'Alpha 3, just going to park close.'

Mark waited for a few minutes while the radio was silent.

'Alpha 3, just walked past and driver was having a cigarette and talking to his friend and saying it was the quickest 50 bucks he has made in a while. Sounds like he has delivered the tape.'

'Alpha 3 can you check the gas station.' Mark barked at the radio handset.

'Alpha 3,' was the acknowledgement on the radio.

Mark was clearly not happy and came and sat at the kitchen table with his hands on his head. He stared straight ahead.

'Well, I think we lost them or at least the tape. Clever move to pull into a garage for the handover. Although the guy's would have noticed if there were stray individuals or cars parked.'

'OK, so we know they got the tape and now we should wait for Emily to call me. It could be some time, even days for them to confirm all the systems work.' I said, trying to find a positive element to the bad news.

Jim sat for a moment and then suddenly jumped up.

'Jon I have all the Fielding project files in the back of my car. I thought I had better not leave them anywhere that could get turned over by the enemy. I'll just go and get them to see if there are any details that might help us.'

Mark followed Jim to his car and was conspicuously holding one hand behind his back and looking down the street in both directions.

Jim came back in with a pile of folders and put them on the dining room table. He pulled out two chairs on one side of the table and beckoned for me to sit next to him.

'Let's start here, with contract stuff.' He said as he sorted through the files.

'Here we are. Let's start from the beginning.'

We sat at the table for some minutes before the radio burst into life.

'Alpha 3.'

Mark took a couple of paces to the radio and picked up the handset.

'Go ahead Alpha 3.'

'Alpha 3, I spoke to the gas station attendant and he remembers the taxi because he just pulled up to pump 1 but did not buy any fuel and did not come in to buy anything. I asked who pulled up at the pump after him. He remembered it was a motorcycle, real sporty number, yellow. He thinks it was a Ducatti.'

'All understood Alpha 3, stand down now. Alpha 2 you monitoring?'

'Alpha 2 understood. Want me to do a quick once over the highways.'

Mark thought for a moment and squeezed the handset again.

'It has been nearly an hour since he left the gas station so that is a huge area, but give it a shot.'

'Alpha 2 checking highways.'

Jim and I continued going through the files, but the contract files did not really give us any new information except the exchange of specifications and revisions. Jim decided to pull out the specifications of the work we were asked to do. In addition to producing some circuit boards to Art's design drawings and rack specification. There were specifications for the mounting of racks and cooling fans that we had to deliver. More or less standard kit for us.

Jim went through the specifications and eventually looked up and said.

'Nothing special here Jon. All the detail

circuits and firmware I already know very well.'

'OK lets give it a rest and have some lunch. Just sandwiches, not sure I can eat much else.' I said as I got up from the table and went over to Mark who was sitting on the floor next to the radio.

'Mark, coffee and a sandwich?'

'Great Jon, No cheese though. Got Tuna?'

'Sure, how about you Jim?'

'You know me Jon, anything is fine.'

I went to the kitchen, made coffee in a cafetiere using my stock of fresh Kenya coffee beans. The aroma of the coffee fresh out of the grinder is nearly as nice as drinking it. I grabbed three mugs, a bowl of brown sugar and small jug of fresh cream and put them on the table.

I then made sandwiches.

'Here we are guy's, Tuna for Mark, ham and cheese for Jim and blue Brie for me, all on brown. Help yourself to coffee. We all need this I think and we could be waiting a while.'

I moved some of the files and put them in a pile on the floor with the exception of the one Jim was reading.

The radio broke our silence.

'Alpha 2.'

'Alpha 2 go ahead.' Mark said as he squeezed the handset.

'I have looked in about a 10 mile radius on all the major roads. No yellow motorcycle.'

'OK Alpha 2, park the plane but stay ready for a call.'

'OK Boss, Alpha 2 out.'

Mark looked at me and put his hands out palms up and with a sigh said.

'Well we tried Jon. We have to hope they will release Emily now. I need to think of a way to get to them. Maybe Emily will know where she was held. I know it is early but I'm going to get some sleep.'

'That's a good idea. Jim and I will take these files in the kitchen and shut the dining room doors.'

Jim and I stayed looking at all the design files until about 09:30 PM and several bottles of Coors beer. We then decided to try and grab some sleep.

∆∆∆

My alarm was still set from yesterday and I woke to its monotonous beep. I showered, dressed and joined Jim in the kitchen.

'The coffee is made and I took the liberty of making some toast and scrambled egg for Mark an I.'

'That's great Jim, I am pleased you are looking after Mark.'

'It was great Jon and he added some of that brown sauce that you Brits use. Great start to the day.' Mark said as he reclined in the dining room with his feet up, grasping his coffee with both hands.

'I have not found anything that Jim is bad at yet.' I said, putting my hand on his shoulder as he sat at the kitchen table, studying some pages from one of the files.

Suddenly Jim banged his fist on the table.

'That is a shipping container spec, I am sure. You know one of the big metal containers they load on trucks and ships.' He stared into space and thought.

'I can remember Art asking me to deliver some brackets and bolts to his house. He then left me with a beer and nuts while he delivered them.'

Jim stared straight ahead again for a while.

'He did not go to his lab so it must have been a customer site. It would make sense that the customer site was close to the lab.'

I looked at Jim for some seconds.

'How do you know he did not go to the lab?.

'Because he rarely left me in his house and this time he said he would be gone for about 20 minutes and left me his keys in case I wanted to go for a walk. Those keys were also to the lab.'

Mark sat up and listened carefully.

'Jim do you remember how long he was away?'

'No. But, I guess it was less than 20 minutes because I would have thought he was late. I would have noticed that. One of my little sensitivities, isn't it Jon.'

I nodded and smiled as I made myself some coffee.

Jim thought and stared at me for a few seconds.

'That would make it about the same radius from Art, house as the McAlester airport, because I used to allow 20 minutes to get to his house by Taxi. Maybe he went to the airport?'

I thought about that idea for all of a second as I was getting tired of sitting around and not doing anything.

'Mark, why don't I fly down to McAlester and just have a walk round the airport, talk to a few people?'

'Not sure I want to have two hostages Jon.' Mark said quickly.

'Hey Mark why would they want me as I am the main person who in their strategy wants Em back. I just feel a bit helpless doing nothing.'

'OK how about I get Alpha 2, Mike, to go with you. Maybe meet you at Riverside and fly down with you. He is also a pilot.'

Jim gave me a concerned look, I know he would like to have gone with me.

'I guess we have to stay here and man the phones and radio.'

Mark nodded at Jim.

'But I know where Jon is coming from. That feeling like you should be doing something. I remember it well from some of my missions. At that time we used to strip and clean our weapons and sharpen knives. I must make some calls, one being home.'

Mark made a couple of calls one of which was one of his, 'expect me when you see me', calls to Ann. Ann had become used to events at a moments notice and while very concerned had known the job that Mark had and was a bit less

risky than the years he spent in war zones.
    I then got on the phone and arranged a plane and filed a flight plan down to McAlester.

CHAPTER 8

I met Mike at the airport. I did not recognise him at first from the description Mark gave me. Right build, wrong clothing.

He came over to me as I opened the door of the Cessna. He was dressed in a grey suit, black shoes and white shirt with no tie, carrying quite a large briefcase. Not quite what I was expecting. I think I saw him in my mind as a hulk wearing combat clothes carrying a rifle. He was not a big man but slim and medium height while clearly being a person you could rely on in a scrap.

'You must be Jon, I'm Mike' He said as he stretched out his hand and gave me a very firm handshake.

'I have to merge into the surroundings, hence the suit.'

I offered him the left seat of the plane and he shook his head.

'Best for you to fly and treat me as a passenger. Just in case someone is watching. Which I don't think they are because I have been wandering round the airport playing business man and asking the odd stupid question.'

'Ok, let's get going!'

I did some quick checks and untied the ropes securing the wings to the ground, then we both climbed into the plane.

It was very quiet at the airport and we got into the air very quickly without any hold up. I headed south and followed the highway down towards McAlester as I had so many times recently. We had decided to fly in about a 5 to 10 mile radius of both the lab and Art's home.

We were looking for large shipping containers that our equipment was designed to fit in and maybe a yellow motorcycle.

We started just doing a 10 mile radius of the airport with nothing that looked like large containers. We reduced the radius and altitude to get a better view but still nothing until we got closer to the airport. The town of McAlester was mainly to the north of the airport and between two main roads. However, to the south and east there were no areas that had containers. This would also be easily 20 minutes from Art Fielding's house. There would need to be an access road for an articulated truck to bring the containers into the site.

Finally we spotted an area to the east of the airport on a road with access to the highway. There were two containers hidden from the road by low trees and bushes. We reduced our altitude and Mike got out some binoculars.

'Jon, don't circle but move the plane further east and at an angle so that I have a clear view through the window rather than overhead. Circling is a bit of a give away that we are looking for something.'

' Ok Mike.'

' That's our target! Two containers, three cars and... a yellow motorcycle.'

Mike took a small camera from his pocket and took a few photographs.

'Shall we land and go in on foot.' I said full of expectation of action.

'No, back home and make a plan that will minimise risk to possible hostages like your Emily.'

Mike took his handheld radio and paused for a

second.

'Alpha 2'

I heard Mark's voice clearly on the radio.

'Alpha 2 go ahead.'

'Alpha 2 positive ID and location, returning to base.'

'Good job Alpha 2.'

Mark sounded really positive that we had located what looked certain to be the containers used to house our equipment, even a yellow motorcycle.

We flew straight back to Riverside airport and returned to the house.

CHAPTER 9

WAR ROOM.

Once back at the house we gathered round the table with coffee. Mike set up a board with white paper and felt tip pens on the table. He sketched the scene we had seen from the plane and I was amazed how much detail he had absorbed in the short time we were overhead.

'Well done Mike and Jon, that is about all the information we need to get a plan together, with a detailed map that I have here.' Mark said with a positive flourish.

Mark collected up the sheet of paper and

pens and put them in his bag.

'OK Jon we will get our team together, process the photos and get a plan together. I also have to contact headquarters to give them a briefing and get them involved.'

Mark and Mike walked towards the door and turned to say. 'Jon, Jim we will be in contact soon, most likely tomorrow, time is critical. Stay positive and by your phone,'

They quickly departed and Jim and I sat in silence for a while.

Jim eventually broke the silence.

'What next Jon?'

I thought for a while and stood up.

'I guess we wait and hope Emily is OK, It's sleep for me, if that is possible. I feel that we are about to get into a situation we are not prepared for.'

'Jim you stay in the guest room, you know where everything is.'

'Ok Jon, see you in the morning, early for coffee.'

Jim shook my hand and put his hand on my shoulder.

'Try to get some rest. Night. You know Mark has all the tricks and skills to get this done.'

We made slow progress getting to bed and

delayed with a scotch on the way, but finally went to bed, to a very restless sleep.

△△△

I woke to the ringing of the phone. I slowly reached over and found the handset.

'Morning Jon.' It was Mark.

'Just thought I would give you a progress report. We had a late night meeting and got together with our FBI friends to decide next steps,' he said in a slow very precise manner.

'Thanks Mark I was not expecting things to move so fast,' I said with some surprise.

'We are moving tonight, with my lads supporting the FBI force. Clearly we want to keep a low profile until then.'

'Very good Mark. Shall I come over later today?'

'No sorry Jon I think it is better for you to stay out of the action, if there is any.'

'I am just concerned that this larger, more government oriented force will not have the life of

Emily as top priority. I know her and can recognise her from a distance. I would like to be there, even if it is in the background.'

'Ok, why don't you fly down with Mike in your plane and Mike will look after you as he has the full briefing with the FBI team who are taking the lead. I will get him to meet you ar Riverside airport at 12:00. He will explain the plan then. But be sure they consider life of a hostage ahead of everything.'

'Ok, good luck Mark.'

'Don't worry Jon we have everything covered, Mike will explain later. Bye for now.'

I explained the situaton to Jim when he joined me for breakfast of toast and coffee.

Jim and I worked out the timing of getting to Riverside and the flight plan. We decided to take the van down to the airport so we could take some drinks to put in the fridge and have a place to talk to Mike when he arrived.

ΔΔΔ

I filed the flight plan and drove to Riverside airport. I removed the tie down ropes from the wings and tail of the Cessna and got some water to wash off the dust from the windshield and windows. After a check of the aircraft I switched on the power and picked up the latest air traffic information and weather from the radio.

It was 11:25 and I was beginning to get some twinges of nerves about the days activities when Mike walked round the wing and waved a greeting. He was carrying a small bag which he handed to me.

'What's this, a picnic Mike?' I said.

He laughed and just said. 'That's your kit, we have a dress code you know.'

Just then Jim drove up to the parking area and strolled over to the plane.

'Hi buddy I didn't think you were going to come and wave goodbye.' I said in a jolly manner.

'Well I thought I would come along and just keep an eye on the plane while you guy's were sorting things out.'

I was about to say that only Mike and I were equiped for the mission when Mike threw me a smile and interjected.

'Great idea Jim, you stay with the plane and keep an eye on it, just in case anyone wants to move it. There will be some FBI guy's in plain clothes pretending to do jobs round the airport.'

Jim looked much happier.

'Very good Jon I will keep a low profile and be ready to help if needed. Do you have a flight plan?'

'Yes Jim in the flight bag with the charts. I have done the pre flight checks.'

Jim got in the plane and started his normal job of getting all the charts folded so our route was easily available, getting the flight plan out and filling in any missing information.

I looked at Mike, but he anticipated my question and said.

'It's fine Jon, Jim can be an extra pair of eyes as he knows the airport really well so will detect anything unusual. He will also allow us to just leave the plane in good hands.'

'Your right Mike, he can do everything with the plane except fly it! That is only because he refused to fly it on our trips.'

There was just time to get coffee from the airport reception and run through the meeting that Mike had attended with the FBI. Mark and his team had been assigned two activities. To identify Emily if seen at the site and to secure the perimeter to prevent possible escape.

We walked back to the plane and Mike got in the back with Jim and I in the front. Mike said he would get in the back so that he could look out of both sides as we got close to McAlester.

The flight down to McAlester was uneventful as we had done it at least a dozen times, but it was a reminder of Dr Fielding who was the start of our troubles.

On approach to the airport, doing a standard approach we could see the small group of containers near the airport, surrounded by trees and an industrial area. This was our target. We could see a couple of cars parked quite close to two of the containers but no yellow motorcycle.

We taxied the plane over near the industrial area but out of sight of the containers and cars.

We left Jim with a radio to monitor our activity and he began to tie the wings down to the rings in the parking area. Mike took the bag out of the plane and handed me a black vest that was at least some protection from small arms fire and had FBI on the back. He also took a rifle out of its case and fitted a telescopic sight. After putting additional items in the pockets of his combat jacket and loading the ammunition into his rifle. He put his rifle over his shoulder and turned to me.

'Ok Jon let's go, stay behind me. Jim you stay in the plane and keep out of sight but keep your eyes open. If you see anything we should know about call on the radio using the call sign Alpha3.'

Jim got in the plane and gave us a thumbs up.

'Good luck guy's,' were his word as we left.

We stayed out of sight of the containers and went round between some trees where Mike pointed at a small group of FBI people hiding behind a pile of timber and building materials. Just then I heard the radio.

'Delta 814'

'Go ahead 814'

'Aircraft parked close to our position, 1 occupant.'

Mike spoke into the radio on his jacket. 'Alpha 2 it's Ok 814, that one is ours'

'814 ok,' came straight back from the radio.

Mike turned and gave me the thumbs up.

We waited and waved to the FBI group. It was some time before another message came through the radio.

'Delta 820 moving in'

There was clearly more than one group of FBI officers as the group near us did not move. Mike signalled me to follow him and we moved from our cover out where we could see the cars and the containers through the trees. Mike found a position by some small bushes and raised his rifle to scan the cars and containers. He pointed over to the left of the cars and whispered.

'Alpha1, Mark is over there.'

'Ok I see him,' I replied.

Just then a loud sound came from just in front of the containers.

'This is the FBI, Come out of the containers.'

Nothing moved. We could see both of the large containers main doors. But then the sound of a gas turbine engine starting came from the second container and exhaust came from the top of the container.

'820 Everyone stay under cover,' came over the radio.

There was movement on top of the nearest container. A metal cylinder appeared. There was a bright flash and crack like close lightening. The blue flame shot out and burnt the trees and grass near where the FBI group was under cover. Mike raised his rifle to look through the scope.

Mike fired and hit what looked like a camera next to the cylinder.

There was another flash and the blue flame took out more trees and bushes near us.

'820 Hit the power container.'

'822 affermative, keep your heads down.'

Mike was using his telescopic sight and handed me a small monocular scope from his jacket. He pointed between the two containers and looking through the scope I could see a smaller container behind the two cars.

'Alpha 2.' Mike whispered into his radio.

'Go ahead Alpha2.' Marks voice came back over the radio.

'There is a third container about 100 yards behind the cars. Over.'

'Ok Mike we see it.'

Just then there was a huge explosion and the power container and it's contents physically moved about 3 or 4 feet to one side, followed by some flying metal and flames and more small explosions. Black smoke now engulfed both containers above about 6 feet.

I looked through the scope at the gap between the two containers at the cars. Still no movement.

Suddenly the door of the small container opened and a man in blue overalls pushed Emily out in front of him towards the cars.

'Mike it's Emily.' I shouted and pointed at the gap between the containers.

'Alpha2, Hostage Emily is out of the small container door.'

'Ok Alpha2 we have them covered.'

The radio then said, '820, Everyone hold your fire, hostage out of small container heading for the cars.'

The man hiding behind Emily was followed by another man who was crouching low so as to stay out of sight behind Emily. They all got into the brown 4 door car and it drove off at speed on the road behind the containers towards the airport buildings and exit.

I heard Mike on the radio explaining to his team and the FBI group that Emily was on the right side of the car with the man in blue overalls in the back.

Mike turned to me.

'Jon don't worry we have all the exits covered. My best men.'

As I looked back at the main container complex, men were coming out with their hand up and being processed by the FBI team.

We left our cover and ran towards the airport buildings. We could just see the car racing across the airfield towards the exit. We could see two figures step out from behind the airport buildings hands raised for the car to stop. A burst of machine gun fire came from the car and the men stepped back.

There was then a single shot followed by a second from the flat roof of the airport buildings. The car slewed to the right towards some fencing and the airport building. The car left the paved road and ran into a drainage ditch and eventually stopped engine still running.

No one got out of the car. We were just too far away to see the situation in the car. A number of FBI and our team were getting the passengers out. It was clear as we got closer that the driver had been shot in the chest. I saw Emily get up from behind the front seat and they laid her on the grass. My heart sank as she looked very limp. Then I saw her arm raise and a medic was clearly looking after her. As I got closer the medic said.

'She will be fine sir, just a lot of glass fragments in her head and neck.' She waved at me before they removed some glass and bandaged her head.

I had to move as the ambulance drove up and they loaded Emily and two FBI men into the Ambulance. One of the FBI men was clearly very serious as they had him on oxygen and there were tubes and fluids provided. I asked if I could go with her to the hospital but clearly there was not enough room.

I asked which hospital as the driver climbed in.

'McAlester Regional is quite close sir.' he said as the blue light and siren started.

Just then Jim had run across from the Cessna to the airport buildings and I explained what had happened.

Mark and his team arrived at the main building and began to pack equipment and I saw Mark greeting Mike and the two snipers that were on the roof.

'You go and make sure Emily is ok.' Jim said.

' I will make the plane secure and get back to Tulsa with Mike and the team.' Mark nodded and shook my hand.

'I hope she is ok Jon, I think it went as well as could be expected.'

'Give my thanks to the team Mark,' I said.

I got a taxi from just outside the airport to the hospital, it was only about 20 minutes until we got to the hospital emergency entrance. Like most emergency areas of hospitals it was quite busy and I followed the signs to the reception desk.

I gave them Emily's details and that she was hit with flying glass. The administrator looked at the information on her desk and said that she had gone down to theatre 2 but will be in for some time.

' You are welcome to wait,' she said pointing to an area in an adjacent corridor.

I found the door that said Theatre 2 and located a comfortable chair in sight of the door.

About 2-3 hours passed and I finally saw a trolley come out of the theatre 2 door and go into an elevator further down the corridor. I was not quite quick enough to find out where she went so I went back to the reception desk and found out that she would be in over night.

'You can have a short visit once she has been made comfortable. What is your name sir?'

'Jon Harrison. I am a close friend.' I replied.

She nodded and commented.

'You are given as one of her contacts. Would you like a coffee while you wait Mr Harrison.'

'Thank you that would be nice.'

'Milk and sugar?' she replied.

I nodded and she lead me to a small waiting room and brought me a coffee.

'I will come and get you when she is ready,' she said with a smile.

I sat and waited and watched the activity for about an hour until a nurse came into the waiting room and said.

'Mr Harrison, she is ready for you to see her now. Please follow me.'

Emily was in a small private room sitting propped up with pillows, bandaged from head to shoulders with only one eye and her mouth visible. She was still wearing her hospital gown.

'Thanks for coming Jon,' she said slowly.

'Sorry you are here because I asked you for help,' I said.

I gently held her hand and she squeezed mine.

'I am very lucky because it was a car windscreen which shatters into small pieces. I will be out tomorrow if the doctor gives me the all clear,' Emily said pointing at the bandaged eye.

'Seems one piece went just through my eye lid and just hit the eye. But they don't think there will be any long term damage,' she said in a positive tone.

'Ok so I will call them tomorrow and pick you up?' I said.

'That would be great Jon,' she said with a smile.

I gave her a gentle kiss and said I would call at about 10:00 tomorrow if everything goes to plan. I gave her hand a squeeze and waved goodbye at the door.

I got a taxi back to the airport and went into the main building to find a phone to call Jim. There were still a few of the FBI team scattered about the building.

I called Jim at home and he answered quickly.

'Hi Jon what's the news,' he said quickly.

I explained Emily's condition and the plan to pick her up tomorrow, all being well.

'So I will fly the plane back tonight and come down in the van tomorrow,' I explained.

' Ok Jon the keys are at the airport desk marked with your name, see you tomorrow.'

I phoned in a flight plan and got the keys from the airport reception desk and walked across the airfield to where the plane was parked. I was soon approached by a man in uniform. I explained my role with the FBI and Mark's team and he asked my name. He then walked away a few steps and spoke on the radio.

'Ok Mr Harrison, need any help with the aeroplane?'

'No it's fine thanks.' I replied.

I went through all the usual rituals of pre flight checks and removing the tie down ropes. I waved to the officer and taxied across the airfield towards the first taxiway.

The flight back was uneventful and I spent the time thinking about the events of the past few days. Riverside was far away from all the activity down at McAlester. I dropped the plane keys back into the office and walked over to my van.

I hardly remembered the drive home and when I arrived I immediately made coffee and proceeded to fall asleep in the armchair. After waking up at 2am I finally went to bed.

△△△

I woke at 8:30 and immediately called the hospital to see if Emily would be allowed home. She had been reviewed and would be released at about 11:00. So I prepared myself to drive down and pick her up in the van. I decided that flying down would not be a good idea as she may need to stop on the way. She could then recline the comfortable front seats or even have a short sleep in the back of the van.

Jim and I talked on the phone and I agreed to have Mark and Jim round once Emily is settled.

The pickup from the hospital was quite easy and Emily wanted to go direct to her house as she only had the clothes she was wearing. She was clearly very pleased to be home and immediately went to change into some more comfortable clothes.

'Jon are you going to stay tonight,' she said.

'Sure , I will make sure you are ok and help with anything you cannot do,' I said.

'I am fine except the eye and maybe changing the dressing,' she said in a confident manner.

We sat and talked about the past couple of days and the people that were holding her. It seems they were as scared as she was. They were all engineers and science graduates except one. He was an ex army man from somewhere that spoke an arabic type of language to others that visited.

'When they knew they were surrounded they wanted to escape but the army man was trying to get them to power up the weapon system. The man in charge and a senior engineer, the driver, grabbed a car and drove me across the airfield towards the exit road. The next thing I knew they had guns out of the windows and were shooting. Fortunately I dived behind the front seats,' she explained.

'The next thing I knew was the glass flying and the car crashing into some trees I think.'

Emily was looking very tired and I suggested that she got some rest and I would sleep on the sofa with a blanket. She went off to get me a blanket and a towel and gave me a kiss.

'Just this once then, you won't get away so easily next time,' she said in a devilish voice.

In the morning I took some toast and coffee to Emily and explained that I had a meeting with Jim and Mark later, but to call if she needed anything.

HARRISON FILES.

Emily waved as I got in the van to drive home.

CHAPTER 10

I woke at 07:30 and was about to call Emily when the phone rang, it was Jim.

'Hi Jon, how is Emily?' he said.

I explained I was going to call her but maybe a bit later when I was sure she had woken up.

'Ok for Mark and I to come over at about 10:00?'

'Yes that's great, I will have the coffee ready!' I said.

I waited until about 9:00 to call Emily. She answered the phone immediately, so she was already awake.

'Morning Em, how are you this morning?'

'I am very much better for a good sleep, but the

eye is very annoying,' she replied.

'You should get them to look at it as soon as possible.'

'Yes, I have an appointment this afternoon at 3.'

'Do you want me to take you Em?'

'No, it's ok Jon my friend is taking me. She is a nurse at the hospital and came up for coffee this morning and was very helpful in changing my dressing.'

I explained that I was having a catch up meeting with Jim and Mark today and would keep her up to date.

'Come over at the weekend and we can catch up then,' she said.

'Ok Em see you at the weekend,' I said.

△△△

Jim and Mark arrived at 10 and I greeted them with a warm handshake.

'Great job, you two! We got Emily back and shut down the energy weapon operation,' I said with enthusiasm.

'Sad about Dr Fielding though,' I said in a more sombre tone.

I made coffee and we sat round in the living room.

Mark gave us a status of the meeting he attended earlier in the morning. It seems that the combined force had indeed shut down and contained the energy weapon threat. It had been planned to export the containers amongst others in a shipment of machine parts on completion. Two of the FBI and reservist team had sustained injuries, but they were not too serious and they were both out of hospital. Mainly bruising and fractures from body armour. The terrorists however, had three fatalities and the rest were detained for interrogation.

'We should not be too complacent though. We know the people at the top of this conspiracy are still out there. The services will be looking for them from information gathered, they will be trying to leave the country. The FBI have both descriptions and even a photograph.'

'More coffee Mark?' I pointed at the coffee pot.

'No thanks Jon, I have to go and finish writing up our reports and delivering all the historical data we collected, to be delivered to the FBI team. You must come over to dinner next week though... and maybe a game of golf,' he said with a chuckle.

'Ok thanks for the update, we will see you soon. I will buy a new box of golf balls!'

He laughed and waved as he left.

'You ok Jim,' I said slowly.

'Sure, just a bit of information for you,' he said quietly with a smile.

'Just as I was locking up the plane, a woman in uniform came over to talk to me. She asked me if Mr Harrison was around. I said that you had gone to the hospital with the hostage. After some time and because she was wearing body armour and FBI uniform I had not recognised her. It was Lorna!' He exclaimed.

Jim continued the story of how she had been monitoring activity at the McAlister airport for some months. When we first met she was not sure about our involvement in whatever was going on at the airport. She soon realised that we were not aware of the activity at the airport, but when Dr Fielding was murdered she knew that he was the connection with the airport. From then onward she could not make contact and was under instructions to withdraw from the immediate operation. She was however, watching us in case things got difficult.

'Jon she really wants to see you again... soon,' he said with urgency.

'Wow, now I understand it all. The questions when we first met and then the silence,' I said with a sigh.

Jim finished his coffee, shook me by the hand and walked to the door.

'Well buddy, that has given you a lot to think about. I will see you soon. I would give her a call,' he said with a wink.

I gave him a wave as he drove off.

ΔΔΔ

It all seemed very normal and quiet compared with the last couple of weeks. I briefly went to the office to pick up the mail and see what deliveries had come during our period of forced absence.

I picked up the post and three or four small packages that had been left in our entrance and put them in the van before going back home.

I had only been home a few minutes when the phone rang.

'Hi Jon it's Lorna,' said the soft voice.

'Hello it's really good to hear from you,' I said quickly.

'I'm so sorry I have not been able to call you. I am sure Jim has explained why by now.'

She explained that she did not really live at the airport and that the house was rented just to provide a base for keeping an eye on suspicious activity at the airport. She did not really know what was going on at the airport until the death of Dr Fielding and conversations we had about our business and relationship with Dr Fielding. It was then that the FBI HQ suddenly got very interested and moved her back into the Tulsa office.

'Jon I would love to come and see you. Maybe continue where we left off,' she said softly.

'What about Saturday night,' I said.

'Yes great, how about 7pm?'

'I look forward to that.'

'Ok byee, don't get into any trouble,' she said.

I had not expected to hear from Lorna and this had given me a new direction of thought. After hearing her voice I was more convinced that she was someone whose company I could really enjoy.

I called Emily to see how her appointment at the hospital had gone. She was very pleased that there was no long term damage to her eye. She also invited me to her house for dinner on Sunday evening about six.

I realised that I would have to tell Emily about Lorna. Sunday would give me time to explain. We had not been together for a long time, one night did not mean we were back together.

My thoughts went back to Saturday night with Lorna. Maybe I would make a sharing meal since we did not say dinner. Shredded Duck with pancakes and plum sauce, would be fun.

The phone rang again and it was Mark inviting me to dinner Saturday. I told him I had Lorna coming over on Saturday night.

'How about Tuesday,' I heard Ann say in the background.

Mark said that they were looking forward to it and would give Jim a call and invite him too.

CHAPTER 11

WOULD THINGS BE THE SAME AGAIN?

For the first time in the last few weeks I slept until 9:30. I made some coffee and decided to have a day tidying and cleaning, as this area of my life had been neglected for some time.

There was only one break from the cleaning. A call from Jim to let me know he would be going into the office Monday and also attending the dinner invite from Mark on Turesday.

By 3pm the house was back to it's normal clean

state. I went to the local supermarket to get all the things I needed for Lorna's visit and the next few days.

I started cooking the duck in the oven very early on low. I was really looking forward to seeing Lorna. At 7:15 the door bell rang and I jumped up and opened the door.

'Hi there, nice to see you again, in normal circumstances,' she said as she stepped through the doorway and gave me a kiss.

'It's nice to see you too, come on in and make your self comfortable,' I said as I gave her a hug and pointed at the sofa.

I took her jacket and saw that she was just as beautiful as I had remembered from our dinner party in her house.

'Wine or something else,' I said.

'Oh yes, a light and fruity red if you have it!'

I went to the utility room where I stored the wine and looked through the labels and spotted one that I thought would fit the description. I opened the bottle and grabbed a couple of glasses from the kitchen. I poured a little into a glass, handed it to Lorna and looked at her for approval. She sipped and nodded with a smile.

We sat and talked about the past two weeks and how she really wanted to ring me and keep me away from trouble. It was clearly difficult for her as she was leading an under cover investigation of Dr Fielding centred around activity at the airport.

She explained that very early in the investigation they had realised that we were not aware of the nature of the project Dr Fielding was involved in. But she was not allowed to let me know her true role, so as not to risk the plans and software getting sent out of the country and the project stopping. While Dr Fielding was following instructions to protect his family he was also clever enough to only give them the minimum information as he delivered each part of the project.

However, as the plasma weapon reached testing phase, they realised his strategy and that is when they took all his computers and equipment. They clearly killed him when he resisted.

But Art had been one step ahead of them and

stored all the critical information to make the system operate effectively on a remote system that Emily and I eventually cracked.

Being very familliar with the critical nature of the data through her defence work, she gave one of her security contacts the original tape and they constructed a replica with critical elements still missing. The conspirators realised that there was still information missing and started following all the people involved to find out who was most likely to have it. They eventually got to Emily and her knowledge of encryption and secure systems and guessed that she had the data.

'Poor Emily was the unfortunate person they took, thinking that she would have the information. I am so sorry that she was used as a lever to get the tape Jon,' she said slowly.

'Fantastic result though, let's eat!' I said pointing at the table.

I topped up her wine and went to prepare the meal. It only took a few minutes and I brought it all in on a tray and placed the dishes in a line on the table.

'It is shredded duck, pancakes with plum sauce

and spring onions. It is help yourself!' I said pointing out each dish.

'Wow that looks great,' she said building her pancake and duck.

Dinner went very well and Lorna explained about her current role and life with the FBI. I offered her more wine, but she declined.

'I have to drive home and in my job drunk driving is unacceptable!'

I looked at her with a smile and said.

' You could always stay here.'

She looked at me with an amused expression.

'But it's only our first date and I did not bring anything with me.'

She looked at me seriously and said.

'No but seriously I am staying in a temporary house set up by the FBI and I have to get back by 11:00. Let's get together in my new apartment when I move in. I really enjoyed this evening and look forward to getting our lives back on a normal footing.'

She stood up and moved round the table towards me arms outstretched. I stood up and put my arms round her waist. She did not delay in kissing me quickly and then a longer more passionate kiss.

'Must go, it was lovely to see you and I will call you when I have moved in,' She said as she picked up her jacket and walked to the door.

She turned and waved as she walked to her car. I waved as she drove off. I felt very positive about the evening and where our relationship could go in the future.

CHAPTER 12

SETTING THE WAY FORWARD.

After a great nights sleep and a lot of thought about Lorna, I began thinking about the meeting with Emily in the evening.

I gave Emily a call and asked her if she was doing anything lunch time.

'Come over for a beer and a sandwich. We can go for a walk as I am a bit short of exercise. We can walk down to the park.'

'Ok that sounds good, oh and how is the eye?' I said quickly.

'Fine but not easy looking like a pirate,' she joked.

'Ok I will come over at lunch time. Bye for now.'

'Bye Jon, see you soon,' she said.

I heard her put the phone down.

I went out in the van at about 11:00 and stopped at a corner store to pick up a few bottles of beer and some chocolates.

As I arrived at the house, Emily was there to greet me at the door. She threw her arms around me and lead me into the house. I handed her the bag with beer and chocolates.

'For me!' she exclaimed.

'Yes, you have done so much and taken risks beyond any expectations, I have heard how you took a chance by giving the enemy false data.'

'That's me, that's how I do things,' she said with

a shrug of her shoulders.

'Come on in and open a couple of beers. We can put all the stress behind us.'

She left the room briefly and returned with a wicker picnic basket.

'I thought it would be nice to have a picnic.'

We finished our beer and we took a picnic blanket and the picnic basket between us out and across the street through a small gap between the houses to an open area with trees. She spread the blanket and we sat down.

We ate the sandwiches she had made, cheese and tomato, ham and pickle.

'What a nice idea to have a picnic. How is the eye feeling?.

'Oh it is fine now, just itches wth this dressing and pirate patch. But it will be off in a couple of days.'

I needed to pick a time to bring up the situation with Lorna. Now seemed like a good time.

'Well what have you been doing since we parted?' I said.

There was a brief gap in the conversation.

'Oh well, my life did change after we had not been together for a while.'

There was another long pause.

'I met someone who made a big change in my feelings. Remember the nurse that took me to the hospital? We are more than just friends. Are you shocked?' she said looking in my eyes.

'Well, yes but it is because of our relationship, even recently we...'

'Yes, I know,' she interupted.

'I still have feelings for you, but not in a loving way anymore,' she said looking into my eyes directly.

'It was a really difficult time for me as I did not understand my own feelings for about a year. Now I am completely ok with how I feel,' she touched her chest and took a deep breath.

'I am so pleased you have found love and happiness. I have thought about you often.'

She smiled and sat up straight.

'What about your life?' she replied.

I told her the story of how I met Lorna and the situation to date. It was beginning to get a chill in the air, so we packed up the picnic and walked back to the house.

'Well Em I am so glad we had this chance to catch up. I hope we can stay in touch.'

'Oh yes, so do I Jon,' she said as she threw her arms round my neck and gave me a kiss.

I waved as I drove off in the van. I had time to

think about Emily and the changes she had gone through. I was relieved that she was happy and I would not need to worry about her being on her own. My immediate focus had to be catching up with all the projects we had at work.

When I got home I called Jim.

'Hi Jon, what's happening? 'he said almost back to his normal level of enthusiasm.

I told him about Emily and how she would make a full recovery. We agreed to go into work and see what needs urgent attention. We agreed to start the week as a normal Monday morning but maybe a bit later at 10:00.

△△△

It seemed like ages since we had spent a normal day at the office. We decided to collect all the material we had as part of the Dr Fielding project and package it up for delivery to Mark for onward delivery to the correct government department. This included printing the emails, drawings, software and quite a few prototype parts and printed circuit boards. It felt quite satisfying when we closed up the large cardboard box and finally labelled it 'Dr Fielding Project'.

Finally we were ready to move on with our lives and business. We were both looking forward to lunch with Mark the next day.

CHAPTER 13

NO LOOSE ENDS.

I picked Jim up from his house and we headed out of town towards Mark and Ann's house. As we approached the electric gates opened and there on the steps at the front of the house were Mark and Ann. As we got out of the van Ann came over and greeted us with a kiss on the cheek. Mark shook our hands.

'Mark I just need to get some business out of the way first.' I opened the van door and took out the large cardboard box.

'Ah yes, I will look after this Jon,' he said and took the box into the house.

Ann took us both by the arm and led us into the house.

'Wine or beer gentlemen,' she said as she pointed to a row of bottles on the kitchen counter.

We both agreed on beer and Ann poured us each a glass. We all sat round a large coffee table on two sofas. Ann then brought in a tray of snacks and potato chips.

'Nice to see you both in one piece and more or less back to normal. I am so glad that Emily is ok and I understand she has no permanent damage,' Mark said as he pretended to wipe sweat from his brow.

'We all got away with very light casualties. Two of my team got minor injuries from bullet impact on body armour, you know, broken rib and some cuts and bruises. One FBI guy got hit but I don't know his status yet,' he said taking a large sip of beer.

'However, the enemy did not do so well. My team had two main roles, to identify the hostage and to secure the perimeter. My two best snipers were on the exit road and they took out the two guys that were driving out with Emily. They were on the roof of the low building near the exit gate and managed to take the shots to avoid Emily in the back of the car.'

'That was a tricky decision and shot,' I said.

'They are the best and have got us out of many difficult situations. I am proud of my team of reservists and retired specialists.'

Clearly Mark had a well tried and tested team that he had developed over a number of years.

'Jon thanks for all your data, I will forward it to the relevant security guys. I also have all the tapes and decoded data from Emily.'

Ann topped up our beer and guided us in to lunch. As usual it was enough for twice the number of people and the meal was well populated by jokes and comments on my golf skills. The beer and wine went on until late and I finally got home by about midnight.

Jim and I were back to our normal routine and I was looking forward to a call from Lorna. I felt very positive about the future and very lucky that I had so many good friends around when I needed them. We had all got a lot closer in this shared experience.

Jim and I would now go back to work with a new energy and caution about what we are getting involved in through our design work.

HARRISON FILES.

Printed in Great Britain
by Amazon